HONOR GUARDS

Guardians of the Fae Realms: Book 10
JL Madore

Honor Guards: Guardians of the Fae Realms

JL Madore -- 1st ed.

ISBN: 978-1-998372-67-6

BEFORE YOU START CHAPTER ONE!
Honor Guards is book two in Honor Thornebane's harem and book 10 in The Guardians of the Fae Realms series.
If you're new to the series and missed the first book of the harem, you'll want to start with book one, Honor Restored. Or all the way at the beginning of the series if you want the intro to how we got here. You can grab the books for the first two harems below and start at book 1 of the entire series.
Guardians of the Phoenix.
Darkness Calls

If you don't want to, that's fine too. The story stands alone, there will be a lot of characters you don't know.
To that end:
Calli is the phoenix, and her guardians are Kotah (Wolf), Jaxx (Jaguar), Hawk (Hawk...obvi), and Brant (Bear)

Keyla is Kotah's sister and her harem came next with Creed (Mind Guardian Fae), Dillan/Doc (Bear) and Rhylan (Dragon)

Hope this helps.
Enjoy,
JL

CHAPTER ONE

Honor

I am Honor Thornebane, Princess of Dornte, a strong mind guardian, and the Guardian of the Crown. I draw a deep breath and steady my nerves. I can do this. Trailing my fingers over the cool stone of the polished wall, I squint my eyes, struggling to adjust to the pitch darkness consuming the chamber ahead of me.

Being in this space sends a shiver of power up my spine. I can't tell if it's my power surging or energy from the Guardian Chronicles coming to greet me.

Either way, my cells are alive with anticipation.

There doesn't seem to be a light switch. Then again, would a secret chamber hidden within the wall of the Guardian's library be wired for electricity?

Something tells me no.

Well, there's not much I can do or learn if I can't see so there must be something here to illuminate my surroundings. I face the wall on my right and run my palms over the surface, searching for anything that could shed light on the situation.

Tundra found the entrance to this private annex and is certain the tools I need to learn about my role as the protector of the crown lay within.

"Does anyone know how to turn on the lights?" I call over my shoulder.

They're all back in the library proper waiting for me to come into my own and be great—my brother... my bestie... the three men I'm seeing.

Holy schmoly... three men.

I'm out of my mind.

I slide my palm against the polished stone wall on the other side of the entrance corridor and find nothing there either.

My boots shuffle along the floor as I shift my weight to step deeper into the room. As a Guardian of the Crown, I grew up knowing I would be bound to three men—a representative from each of the Dornte quadrant biomes—the desert planes, the snowy peaks, and the forested jungle.

Taking them into my bed isn't mandatory.

Partnering with them is.

After studying the way my mentor did things, I've decided to focus my reign by doing everything the opposite way. She chose her civilian lover over her biome generals.

I wouldn't do that—not even for Lukas.

After he spent weeks breaking the curse of the Blood Witch and brought me out of my catatonic state we were linked. Bound. Then, when Tundra and Dune showed up, I couldn't just walk away.

Lukas is part of me.

Thankfully, having spent the past months watching Calli and the Guardians of the Phoenix and then my brother Creed during his mating, Lukas was open to a polyamorous union.

And how sexy is that?

Seriously, he's been so good about things. Understanding. Logical. Mature. Supportive.

I wonder how he'll feel if the third general shows up.

Where is the general for the forested jungle?

Add that to the list of important questions that need answering. Along with, how do I revive the Amberloq forces? How do I stop the goblin rebellion and take down the man at the top of the dung heap, Ruic Breard? How will the union I have with Dune and Tundra change me? Oh, and a million other questions.

"How's it going in there, Princess?" Dune asks.

"It would be better if I could see. Does anyone know how to turn on the lights in here?"

"The chamber is built to respond to you," Tundra says. "You are the Guardian of the Crown. Connect with the magic of the room and command it."

Command it? Easy for him to say.

Still, if Lukas is the go-to guy for all things magic and strategy, Tundra is the source of knowledge for all things Amberloq. He is a dedicated soldier and a devout follower of the canon.

"Command it," I whisper, turning to press my palms against the wall.

Another surge of energy tingles through my fingers, across my hands, and up my arms. "Let there be light."

I push my intention into the wall and envision the room responding to my will.

My surroundings are flooded with a warm, golden glow. I scan the room, studying the coffered ceiling above, and then take in the rest of the small, rectangular space. "Lights are on. Good one, Tundra."

If they respond, I can't hear them. My entire focus has shifted to understanding where I am.

The walls are constructed of massive sheets of polished onyx. They seem to be solid black but with the golden light dancing across the surface from above, I can see flecks of gold and silver flickering in the dense blackness of the stone.

The room is about seven feet deep and twelve feet wide with floor-to-ceiling cabinets on the two end walls and a console and desk chair in the middle.

I slide the chair out from under the desk and take a seat. Studying the surface of the console, I finger the slot that seems to beg for something to be inserted into it.

I chuckle. "Rude but yeah. What do you want me to put in your slot?"

I eye up the cabinets to my left and right and make my way over. There are no handles on the front, but when I press my palm on the right door, a soft *click* releases the panel and it swings open.

"There you are." The cabinet is filled with rows and rows and rows of jade tablets.

There are no dates or subject headings to help me decipher what's on the tablets, just a rune or pictograph, and a number. I reach for the number one tablet with what looks like an open book. It's in the top left of the cabinet, so I'm hoping it's the starting point.

Taking it over to the console, I turn it so the number and picture are in my palm and slot it in. The moment it locks into place, a rush of energy sweeps through the room and the hair on the nape of my neck stands on end.

I should be alarmed when the door slams shut but am too fascinated to worry about that right now.

"Welcome Guardian," a voice says as the wall opposite the desk lights up with projected images. "The disc you have chosen is the first in a series of recorded history called the Chronicles of the Amberloq. They have been recorded to guide the Guardian of the Crown through her transition of becoming a leader of the royal military force."

"Recorded by who?" I ask.

The bodiless voice doesn't appear to be sentient or able to answer because she keeps talking.

"—as you, too, will record important thoughts and discoveries to be studied by those who follow you."

That heightens my interest. Did my Aunt Valorous leave me instructions?

Reality hits and that bubble of hope is popped. She moved her army out of this house and off the castle grounds more than a decade ago. There's no way she could've explained to me what was happening at the time of the raid or after, while she was in captivity.

I'm no closer to knowing how to fix this.

"Fine. Many other Guardians came before Valorous. She dropped the ball on being my mentor, but I have all these other discs to learn from."

"—each Guardian chooses a symbol or picture to represent their reign and their personality. Blank discs can be created…"

I stop listening to the instructions and get up to look around again.

"Each picture represents a Guardian of the Crown from the past and the information and wisdom they wished to impart."

That's cool.

I leave the first disc running in the background and go back to study the archived tablets with a keener eye. There are ten discs with the same open book on the spine as the one I chose.

Obviously, the book stands for learning something.

Then, the next run of discs has a dagger. There are seventeen of them before the picture on the spine changes and there's a dragon… and then a faery… and so on.

"Okay, I think I get it." I bypass the console as I cross the room and open the cabinets on the other side.

More discs are set in the same rows. Eight with a funky battle helmet, and then eleven with a tree, and then nine with a shield….

"What symbol will represent me?"

I have no idea and the narrator doesn't answer. She

continues to drone on about the importance of passing on information to the legacy warriors to come.

"Trust me, I get that. These discs are going to be the only thing that get me through any of this. Thank the gods someone had the foresight to do this because my mentor bailed and failed."

I finish scanning the cabinet and find dozens of blank discs in the bottom rows, which I assume are yet to be filled.

"Okay, a good first day. Maybe I'm not completely screwed after all. I still have a long way to go, but at least I've got a road map."

〜

Lukas

Honor's been in the Guardian's private chamber a long time. While I don't feel like anything heinous is going on, I'm worried. Valorous left her unprepared for what's to come. Laryssa and the Blood Witch tore her down even further.

Not that I'm worried she won't rally and be the best Guardian of the Crown this quadrant has ever seen—I know she will—what worries me is the pressure she puts on herself.

She's so driven not to disappoint her brother or let down the citizens that I'm afraid she'll overdo it. With her physical and emotional states weakened by the trauma of the past two years, she needs to take things slow and build up to greatness.

A phone rings and it seems to break the collective breath everyone is holding.

"He's what?" Keyla says, lifting her hand to her mouth as she listens to the caller speak. "Is it permanent? Is there damage we missed?"

The rest of us turn to find out what's going on.

She frowns and shakes her head. "No. I'm not saying you did

6

anything wrong, sweetie. You know that. I just don't understand how this could happen."

Hawk, Brant, Jaxx, and Kotah curse and share a round of grieved glances.

Creed tears his gaze from Keyla and looks at Kotah and the other wildling shifters. "What? You can hear the other side of this conversation, am I right? What's happening?"

"Oh, I'm so sorry." Keyla pulls the phone from her ear, taps the screen, and holds it in front of her. "Doc, I put you on speaker. Let me catch everyone up."

"Yes, please," Creed says. "Dillan? Are you all right? What damage? Are you hurt?"

Keyla shakes her head. "No. Not him. Shadow is awake, and while his tests came back indicating that everything is working properly, for the moment, he's blind."

Shit.

I sigh and perch against the edge of the table against the wall. "Could it be temporary, Doc? Maybe swelling or something that will resolve over time?"

"There's no way of knowing at the moment. From what I can tell, his vision shouldn't have been affected at all. If cracking his head on the car door was the cause, there's no reason why he'd lose his sight in both eyes. It makes no sense."

"What can be done?" Hawk asks. "Do you need equipment? Specialists? How do we turn this around?"

"I'm not sure it has anything to do with us. His hydroxyecdysone levels are through the roof and there's no way that is from a crack to the head."

"What do hydroxy-whatever levels do?" Bear asks.

"In nature, hydroxyecdysone is the amino acid that triggers the production of a hormone from neurosecretory cells in the brain."

Brant widens his eyes and growls. "Stop talking doctor,

asshole. Tell us what the fuck you're saying. What do these amino acid and brain cells trigger? Just spit it out."

"Metamorphosis. In wildlings, insects, and other animals that metamorphose from one state into another, increased levels of hydroxyecdysone imply a changing of state."

"Changing to what?" Keyla asks, looking as confused as the rest of us. "He's an urban elf, what is there for him to change into?"

"I'm not sure, babe," Doc says on the other end of the phone. "All I know is the guy's eyes are blank and glittering like two opals. Everything else seems the same, but he's only been awake for twenty minutes. I have no idea what we'll find in an hour or beyond that."

Keyla sinks against Creed's chest as he gathers her in for support. "Okay. We're at a bit of a standstill here helping Honor. When we figure out what's happening, we'll come straight back to help."

"No rush. I've got things covered medically, but I thought you'd want to know because he's understandably freaked out and could likely use a friend."

"Thanks, hon. We'll be back soon." Keyla ends the call and slides the phone back into her pocket.

"You should go," I say, pushing off the edge of the desk. "Honor's in no danger, the castle brownies are helping with the restoration of the house, and Shadow needs a friend. If you guys want to return to the King's Tower, we'll take care of what's happening here and check in later."

Keyla checks with Creed and they ready to leave.

Calli meets the questioning looks of the rest of the quint and shakes her head. "I'm staying. Whatever is happening in that room is monumental for my bestie. I'm not leaving."

Keyla nods. "That's fine. Creed, you should stay and see what Honor discovers in the chamber. I'll head back."

"Not alone you won't," Creed says. "Not when goblins attacked Honor just the other night."

"I'll walk you," Kotah says. "Shadow has always been good to us. I'd like to show him my support in a difficult time."

Jaxx and Hawk decide to go back too.

I'm torn. As much as I'm curious about what Honor has found in her hidden room, she's in no immediate danger. Shadow and I got close in the past month while we tended to Honor. I like him... a lot.

Maybe a little too much considering my current situation. Right. That makes my decision for me. If I were to go, it would be out of misplaced affection. I'm with Honor now and by extension have pledged myself to Tundra and Dune.

My place is here.

"I want to be there when you interrogate Hunter," I say, pegging Hawk with a look. "I'm serious. If you go back there and can't help Shadow, your first instinct will be to take control of something else. Wait for me."

Hawk flashes me a toothy grin. "Maybe you don't know me as well as you think you do."

"Like fuck. Hunter made inroads with the goblins who want Honor dead, I want a crack at him. Don't fuck with me on this, Barron."

Hawk holds up his hands in surrender. "Fine. I'll check with Rhylan and make sure my baby brother's being a good captive but it won't go any further than that."

Good. That's fine.

Tundra

It's a shame that Shadow is suffering again. The man has had a run of injury and assault. I regret shooting him with a tranquilizer when we first arrived. Then there was the violent car accident while avoiding the missile attack on the way to the war memorial, and now this.

I can't imagine waking up in a recovery bed and finding myself unable to see. I would lose the ability to fight, to perform my duties as an Amberloq warrior, and worst of all... I wouldn't be able to fly.

I can't imagine the horror of that.

Perhaps for Shadow, sightlessness is not as devastating. He's not a warrior, his duties don't take him into hostile, combative situations, and he doesn't fly.

I don't truly understand what royal counselors do. Is it his job to sit and listen to people unburden their troubles? If so, he can still do that. He can sit with someone and offer sage advice without his eyesight.

Perhaps it's not as dire as Doc fears.

"Princess," Dune says, jumping up from sitting on the window ledge sometime later. He's been remarkably quiet up until this point and I follow his line of sight to find Honor exiting the Guardian's library.

She looks well.

That's an understatement. She is a stunning and strong warrior and carries herself with the grace and elegance of her station as the Princess of Dornte.

She is breathtaking.

And by some miracle of destiny—she is mine.

"How was that?" Lukas rushes to get a supportive hand around her. "Are you all right?"

I don't blame him. As strong and capable as Honor is, her confinement over the past two years as well as her inactivity while locked in that lead vault has left her physically drained.

It will take time to build up her stamina once again.

"I'm fine," Honor says, smiling at us. "More than fine. There is an entire library of information as well as advice from previous women who held the position before me. Even with Valorous's lack of foresight, I now have hope I'll be able to study hard and make a good leader regardless."

"That is wonderful. Congratulations, Princess," I say. "A weight lifted off your shoulders, I'm certain."

"Yeah, really great, girlfriend," Calli says. "We're all so happy for you."

She scans the faces in the room and frowns. "Then why do you all look like someone died?"

Calli waves that away. "No one died. But, as much as we hate to ruin your triumphant moment, there is something sad and serious going on."

Honor stiffens and stands taller. "Tell me."

Shadow

I've never considered myself a coward—until now. Lying in this bed, with my world around me nothing but a void of darkness, I am truly afraid. What if Doc's optimism is misplaced and this isn't temporary? What if the car accident destroyed something vital within my head and left me blind for the rest of my life?

How do I manage that? How do I counsel people on navigating through diversity when all I want to do is sink deeper into this mattress? Mayhap this is the universe's way of expanding the breadth of my understanding so I might be a better counselor and guide.

If it is, I would rather fall short as a counselor.

Mayhap if I go back to sleep and wake up again, this will have all been a dream.

A nightmare.

"Shadow. I'm here." Warm fingers brush over my hand as

Princess Nakeyla's presence settles over me. "Doc told me what's happened. How can I help?"

"Do you know how to restore my sight?"

"I wish I did. Hawk spoke to Doc about the equipment we might need to be brought through the gate and Creed is speaking to Rhylan right now about who in this realm might be able to help."

"That's right," Doc says, coming in to join us. "Maybe it's something I missed or the swelling from the trauma of the accident hasn't dissipated enough. There could be a dozen reasons why your vision is altered."

"It is not altered," I say, gripping the coverlet folded over my lap. "It is no longer functioning." At. All. "I have no sense of light in the room around me, no movement, nothing. I am experiencing a complete visual deficit."

"At this moment," Doc says. "Creed is putting me in touch with the people in this realm who might help me figure out what's happening. It's not time to panic yet."

Not time to panic?

I am blind!

Someone sets a hand over my wrist and squeezes. A rush of reassuring energy soothes the ragged ache in my soul and I draw a deep breath. "Your Majesty."

"I am here, Shadow," Kotah says. "You don't face this alone, my friend."

"Kotah's right," Keyla says. "This is a momentary setback. You hit your head. Once the swelling goes down everything will go back to normal. You'll see."

I doubt that, but I have no strength to argue.

Dune

"I get that it's unfortunate Shadow is blind, but what does that have to do with us? Everyone's acting like it's them who is suffering. What's with that?"

Tundra turns a severe scowl on me and then checks the room and over his shoulder as if he's afraid someone heard. "The man is part of the royal court, he is a personal friend of both the Wolf King and our queen, and is the confidante of our princess."

"I know all of that," he whispers, stepping closer, "but that has nothing to do with us, does it?"

"Directly, no. But if you consider Honor's feelings and Queen Keyla's happiness as part of your duty, then yes, I'd say it has a great deal to do with all of us."

That sounds like a lot of Tundra double-talk for 'everything is our duty'. I swear he truly believes everyone is safest when they're tucked under our wings.

But I don't want everyone tucked under my wings.

I check over my shoulder to ensure no one else can hear me. "It's bad enough that Honor has feelings for a man who's not even Elbirfae or even a Biome General. Lukas has already been added to our lives. Now we're supposed to care about the elf too?"

"As a living being whose life entwines with our own? Yes, we're supposed to care."

I sigh. "Well, I don't."

"That is because you're fundamentally selfish and self-centered."

"I disagree, but don't want to argue."

"Argue about what?" Honor says, stepping out of the library with Creed, Lukas, Calli, and Brant.

"About who is claiming the turret room on the third floor," Tundra says. "It's got a lovely view and once it's cleaned up, it will be a coveted space."

I'm impressed.

I didn't know Tundra could lie so effectively.

"Are you two ready to return to the castle?" Honor asks, her guileless gaze taking in the two of us. "We're all walking back together. The brownies are set here and excited to get to work. I've never seen a group of individuals so excited about silt and cobwebs."

Tundra chuckles. "Well, this place has plenty of both so their passion for hard work will be rewarded."

"That it will," she says studying the roofline and corners as if searching for more of the same. "You can come or stay, but we're heading back now. I want to check in with Shadow. He was there when I woke up and my life had been altered without my consent. I want to return the favor and make sure he knows we're all here for him."

"Of course," I say, stealing a page from Tundra's book and playing the sensitive card. "Shadow's a great guy and he's been a true friend to you. We should absolutely be there for him in his hour of need."

Tundra rolls his eyes behind Honor, but I don't care.

Women aren't that hard to figure out. They want a strong, confident man to comfort and support them, they want to be heard, and they want to be pleasured.

I'm the man for the job.

I've got this general thing in the bag. Honor already thinks I'm cute and charming and I haven't even warmed up my A-game yet.

Lukas comes back from checking on something and nods. "All right. Rhylan sent a couple of escorts through the forest to keep an eye on things. It doesn't look like any goblin surprises are waiting for us in the forest. Time to take our leave."

Sounds good to me. The sooner we get back to the suite, the sooner we can return to the topic of serving our princess the way she deserves to be served.

Honor jogs back over to the library wall to test that the door to the chamber is secured. When she pulls her hand back, she frowns and wipes her fingers on her pants. "I'm ready."

Lukas holds out his arm and she slides in against his side as we leave. "It might be a bit of a fixer-upper at the moment, but something tells me that the next time you step inside this mansion, it's going to be well on its way to being fully restored."

Honor allows the human to guide her toward the front entrance. Before she exits the door, she turns back and smiles at the interior of our future home base.

"Goodnight, Amberloq Hall, and welcome back."

CHAPTER TWO

Honor

We return to the castle in a group of mixed emotions. Everyone is excited about my discovery in the Guardian's Library and yet solemn because of the news about Shadow. I suggest Tundra and Dune take the out and go back to our suite but they decide to join Lukas, Brant, Calli, and me in the King's Tower.

Tundra doesn't like the idea of being separated from me in case another goblin attack breaks out.

He is a sweet and considerate man.

A gentle giant.

Dune agrees, but I think he just doesn't want to be shown up. I haven't figured out who Dune is under all the bullshit, but I'm not giving up.

Keyla meets Creed and me at the entrance to the great room. She looks terribly sad and once again, I regret judging her so harshly over the past weeks.

Creed said she's incredibly empathetic and omega sensitive like her brother. I can tell she's not only worried about a friend but is burdened with his pain and suffering the same way she was with mine.

And I was an uncharitable bitch about it.

Today is a new day.

Thankfully, the longer I'm home and grounded in reality, the more I'm getting over myself. I'll make it right with Creed and build a relationship with his mates.

Except for Rhylan... he can kiss my ass.

"How is he?" Creed asks, pulling Keyla against his broad chest for a hug.

"Kotah's in with him now. My brother is so much better at filtering through the pain of others than I am."

"Do you mind if I go back and see him?" I ask.

Creed smiles at me over Keyla's long, chestnut hair. "Of course not. This is and will always be your home. You never have to ask to be here."

Lukas chuckles. "But you may want to keep to the main floor for surprise visits. I learned that the hard way with the quint."

Creed laughs and Keyla's cheeks flush pink. "Ah... yeah, that's probably best."

"I'll remember that. Thanks."

I leave Lukas and my generals with Calli, Creed, and Keyla and venture to the guest rooms at the back of the suite. Once upon a time, the room Shadow is in was my childhood playroom.

I must've held a million teddy bear balls in here.

It's crazy, but I can't remember what it felt like to be that little girl. I'm not sure when I lost touch with her, but I can't feel her anywhere within me.

When bad things happen, does the trauma destroy that part of you or simply bury it beneath the rubble of life's fallout?

I rap my knuckles against the doorframe and step into the room. Kotah is sitting on the edge of the bed holding Shadow's wrist. It seems intimate, but as I step closer, a rush of serenity washes over me and I realize the true meaning of their connection.

The Wolf King is easing Shadow.

"I'm sorry to interrupt," I say, suddenly unsure that I should've come in. "I wanted to check on you and say how relieved I am you're finally awake."

Shadow swallows and glances my way.

It's terrible to say, but I'm glad he can't see my reaction because I flinch without meaning to.

His eyes are truly eerie.

Not unlike Creed's.

"That is kind of you, Princess," Shadow says. "I was relieved to hear you and the others escaped the accident unharmed."

Shadow has a kind soul and a suave grace. His demeanor comes partly from him being an urban elf and partly because of his natural personality and training.

He's beautiful inside and out.

With his deeply tanned skin, dark purple hair, and the point-tipped ears of his race. He's never hard to look at. In fact, I've caught many people taking notice of him as we walk through the castle together.

Women and men.

"I was deeply concerned about the baby but Dillan assures me both Calli and child are doing well."

"They are. Calli's waddling more every day and eating everyone out of house and home, but all is well."

"A true blessing to be celebrated."

It's not a surprise that even in his hour of emotional upheaval, Shadow is concerned about the rest of us.

Drawing closer to the bed, I sit and take his hand. "Yes, we're all fine. It's you we're worried about."

Kotah shifts on the other side of the bed and stands. "I shall leave the two of you to visit. I hope I have been of some comfort, Shadow. And, of course, if you need me, let Keyla know and I shall return."

"Thank you, Majesty, but you have a realm to run and I am merely one citizen suffering momentary misfortune. Your time is better spent elsewhere, I am sure."

Kotah pats Shadow's shin as he rounds the foot of the bed. "Time spent with friends is always time well spent. Strength and serenity, my friend."

"Gratitude, sire."

Kotah offers me a kind smile and heads out of the room. Like his sister, he seems incredibly young to hold a position of such importance. Also, like his sister, he seems to be managing exceptionally well regardless of his age.

I think back to when I was nineteen and there is no way I would've accepted that kind of responsibility with the same confidence and grace.

I judged them because they didn't have wars to live through to teach them how to lead people in troubled times. I was the one who had things to learn, not them.

"Forgive me," Shadow says, squeezing my hand. "Is everything all right, Princess?"

I snap out of my reverie and focus on the here and now. "You don't need to ask about me, Shadow. You're going through enough turmoil of your own."

"Honestly, I would welcome a conversation about something other than my current state. What kept you so quiet just now? What's been happening with you these past days?"

"Are you sure you want to hear it? It seems petty and trite next to your situation."

"I do. To focus on someone else's troubles would be a welcome distraction. Tell me what happened from the accident onward. I want to catch up."

I proceed to tell Shadow about the car wreck when Lukas swerved so we wouldn't be blown up by the incoming missiles.

Then, how we evacuated and regrouped and how Keyla and Doc had a triage center awaiting casualties in a local restaurant.

"It was there I first saw the strength of Keyla's compassion. Then, when we answered a cry for help and were ambushed, I saw the strength of her courage."

"You were attacked?"

"Yes, Ruic Breard hired local riff-raff and street bandits as his rebel forces. After we were lured out of the restaurant and into a courtyard, enemy men hemorrhaged from the shadows, and Keyla, Lukas, and I barely made it out of there alive."

"Where were your generals?"

"Dune was helping Calli with another group moving in, and Tundra returned from evacuating Creed and came to our aid shortly after. As the Guardian of the Crown, our first duty was to secure the queen and evacuate her to safety. Lukas and I hunkered down and I sent Tundra to take Keyla to our fallback location."

"It sounds harrowing."

"It was. It was my first day on the job and we had to air evac both Creed and Keyla to get them to safety."

Images flood my mind at what happened next.

When Tundra left and Lukas and I faced the danger alone... things ratcheted up for us.

The adrenaline.

The need to feel alive.

The enclosed space of our hiding spot...

I swallow as my heart rate picks up and my core pulses in heated memory. That moment is etched into my cells—the rough brick against my back, the thrust and glide of being pinned as Lukas filled me, the desperation we shared as I clutched his shoulders and bit back my orgasm to keep from giving away our position.

It was one of the sexiest moments of my life.

Shadow arches a brow and offers me a knowing smile.

"Intense situations can bring about intense emotional responses."

Right. Heightened elven senses. Oops.

"I know you warned Lukas away from a relationship with me—"

He lifts his hand. "My concern had nothing to do with either of you making a wrong decision. It was solely to give you time to find your footing. I respect Lukas a great deal and think he will prove to be an asset to you and your quest to find your place."

I exhale. "I'm glad you think so because I think I'm falling in love with him."

"Lucky him," Shadow says, smiling. "What about Tundra and Dune? How do they feel about your relationship with Lukas?"

I tell him about the whole kafuffle about Lukas not being an Amberloq warrior and how I thought I had to toe the line at first. "But that didn't work for me. Lukas is an amazing military man in his own rite, and I want him at my side."

"And your Biome Generals?"

I think about the sex the four of us shared when we agreed to unite as one force. It was fun and I think it brought us all a little closer but...

"If I'm being honest, I don't have the same emotional connection with Dune and Tundra that I do with Lukas. There's something there... but it's not as deep."

"It's early days yet, Princess. Right now, you're adjusting to being back in the realm and learning about your role as leader of the Amberloq. Your relationships with your generals will grow into what they are meant to be with time."

"That's fine for the personal stuff, but we need our relationship as fellow warriors to fall into sync faster than that. With a male like Ruic Breard behind the rebellion threatening the realm, we need to pull our forces together and ready to fight."

Shadow shifts in the bed and rolls onto his side to face me.

"And what of the third general? Has there been contact from the warrior leading the forested jungle?"

The chaos in his mental energy has dissipated remarkably since I arrived. He is so much more relaxed.

Me confiding in him truly does help him.

"No. Nothing yet. With everything happening so fast, we haven't made a prioritized list of what needs to be done. We need to send an envoy to the forested biome and determine the status of their leadership."

He nods. "A sound idea. Now, what of your training? How is that going?"

I chuckle. "Are you sure you want to hear all this? Aren't you tired? I can come back in the morning."

He waves that away. "From what I was told, I have slept for days. No, if you can spare the time, I am enjoying this catch-up very much."

"Me too. And yes, I can spare the time." I sit back, getting more comfortable, and settle in to keep him distracted for as long as he needs.

Lukas

My wrist vibrates with the notification of the incoming text, and I raise my arm to read it at the same time Dune and Tundra read theirs. *Having a great chat and keeping Shadow's mind off things. Feel free to head back to the suite. I'll meet you there later.*

"Good. That's good." I finish my drink and rise from the couch to take my empty glass to the bar. "Honor says she and Shadow are having a great chat session so we shouldn't wait for her."

Keyla grins. "Excellent. I'm glad the two of them get along so well."

"Why?" Dune asks, a definite edge to his voice.

Keyla blinks but doesn't miss a beat. "Because Honor is going through a lot with her transition from prisoner to leader of the crown warriors. Shadow is an amazing counselor and having the two of them connected gives them both a chance to heal and strengthen."

Creed leans close and kisses her cheek. "Insightful as ever, Little Wolf."

I'm not sure if they didn't pick up on Dune's attitude or if they are being polite by not drawing attention to it, but I did, and so did Tundra.

What's his problem now?

Honestly, that would take too much time and energy to figure out. "If someone could assure Honor gets back to the suite safely, I'd like to meet with Rhylan and Hawk and start the interrogations. Hunter and the goblin you captured after the attack have the insight we need to be proactive instead of reactive on the rebellion front."

Creed stands to walk me out. "Don't worry about Honor. I'll ensure she gets back unharmed."

"That is kind of you, sire," Tundra says, "but also unnecessary. Dune and I are pleased to wait for your sister for however long she takes. If we are intruding, we can wait in the hall."

Keyla grunts and waves that idea away. "We're not making you wait in the hall. You are part of Honor's life now and, by extension, ours. If she hasn't come out by the time we're ready to retire, you are welcome to stay here and drink all Creed's liquor."

Creed grunts a laugh. "The queen has spoken."

I say my goodbyes and leave them to sort that out.

It's getting late and the staff and citizens of Thornebane Castle have all but finished their day. I make my way from the King's Tower to the other side of the castle and down to the basement.

After stopping at the new security access doors we installed, I set my hand on the scanner and key in my access code. The door releases and I step through.

When I arrive outside the war room, I can tell there's trouble even before going inside.

"What now?" I scan Rhylan, Hawk, and Jaxx's scowling faces.

Rhylan points at the screen and I'm facing— "Wow, that man is f-ugly as fuck."

"No argument," Rhylan says, his voice more growl than words. "Goblins aren't attractive to begin with but Ruic Breard tips the ugly scale beyond that."

"And then he opens his mouth," Jaxx says, "and he gets uglier still."

I point to the screen which seems to be displaying the type of scene you'd see at an American political rally. There's a large, seated crowd, massive banners, a guy pontificating at a podium. "So, what's with the press conference? Is he running for office?"

"He says he is," Rhylan snaps. "Forget the fact that Dornte is a sovereign kingdom. He says he's opposing Thornbane rule."

"Can he do that?"

"No." Rhylan taps on his tablet and turns off the sound. "That's what worries me. He's putting this out into the quadrant when he knows he has no legal right to call for change the way our laws are structured. Why?"

Hawk frowns. "In my experience, you never have to wait long to find out."

I draw a deep breath and think about this strategically. "Your first step should be to round up your royal litigators and review the foundation of your government laws. If he's got his eye on a loophole, it's better to find it and plug it before he slips through."

Rhylan taps a few lines onto his screen and checks back with me. "You said the first step. What else? I'm a warrior. I'm not savvy in political bullshit."

Hawk looks at me and we start to brainstorm...

"The citizens are loyal to Creed," I say, starting us off. "He'll try to discredit him and his decisions."

"Maybe our first instinct was right all along, and he'll hold the realm hostage financially. He owns the minting contracts for Dornte currency."

"Agreed." I gesture to Rhylan holding his tablet. "Also have your legal department review the agreements for currency production and look for a way to oust Ruic or terminate the contract of Breard Industries."

Hawk nods. "The two most powerful ways to take over a country are by physical force or by fear. Thanks to Hunter and my father's illegal guns, they have the physical force. And judging by what we know of him, I'm guessing the fear tactics we've already seen are just the beginning."

"What do you anticipate?"

He shakes his head. "He'll point out that the Thornbanes aren't strong enough to fend off an enemy attack."

"But they are the ones who attacked."

"Yeah, it's fucked up but it's what's coming. They'll claim the royal family and its warrior force is in shambles and that only he can keep the citizens safe."

"That's not hard to prove when the Amberloq consists of three warriors," I add.

Hawk nods. "Creed took credit for opening the portal gate to the Human Realm. They'll twist that and say he allowed large quantities of illegal guns to get into the quadrant."

Rhylan frowns. "That was them too. Not us."

"Won't matter."

Rhylan growls. "How can it be Creed's fault if they didn't even bring them through the gate he established?"

I nod. "They'll find a way to pin it on him, but the other gate is a good point. We need to find the other access point and shut it down."

"We also need to find out where they are storing the guns," Hawk says. "Hunter will be able to help us there."

I chuckle. "Not willingly, he won't. We'll have to dose him."

"Agreed. And if you feel the urge to rough him up, you have my permission."

"All in the name of public safety," I say, chuckling.

Hawk grins. "Exactly. That's us, making friends and influencing people."

I think about that and my mind barfs up a dozen more scenarios, each worse than the one before. "We need to hammer out contingencies for economic strong-arming. Breard was only the top man of five figureheads in this rebellion, right?"

"That's right," Rhylan says.

"Well, we need a complete jacket on each of the others if we're going to get in front of this."

"What do you need?"

"Net worth, the reach of their power, who they influence, and what they control. I have a bad feeling."

"What do you mean?"

I shake my head. "Let me look at the intel before I start spouting off about the sky falling. Send the files for all the one-percenters involved to Honor's security dropbox and we'll start picking our way through it."

Hawk meets my gaze, and I can see that he's coming to the same conclusions I am.

We've been doing this long enough we can see what's coming a mile away.

And if we're right... it's going to suck.

CHAPTER THREE

Tundra

It's after ten when Doc, Keyla, and Creed turn in and head upstairs, and Calli and Brant leave to go back to the Auburn Suite. Dune and I wait for Honor in the great room of the King's Tower and I have to say, life has taken an unexpected turn. Two years ago, I was an obedient, dedicated cog in the Amberloq wheel.

Now I'm the Biome General of Snowy Peaks and on the cusp of creating a lasting relationship with Princess Honor, the current Guardian of the Crown.

The Powers have bestowed upon me a great honor.

Of course, Dune would argue it had nothing to do with the celestial powers and it is him I should thank.

Dune's place in all this is a mystery to me.

If everything truly does happen for a reason, I don't understand why the universe put Dune in charge of the Desert Planes Biome.

I understand it's a case of appointment by process of elimination, still, it's hard to fathom the universe chose him as the best man for the job.

"Oh, my gods, have you seen all the information being downloaded into our file library? What the slecking hell? Does the human think we're going to read all that?"

I hadn't seen it, so I pull out my tablet and scan through the files. "These are obviously important, and if I'm reading them correctly, they are detailed profiles on Ruic Breard and his allies in the rebellion."

Dune makes a face at me. "I can read. My point is, this much information is overkill."

"Information is power," I say, taking a cursory look at the intel. "If Rhylan sent us this, it's because we need to familiarize ourselves with our enemies. To know them is to anticipate their movements and tactics."

"Whatever." Dune rolls his eyes. "You be the bookworm warrior. I'll be the guy who excels in battle."

His short-sightedness is alarming.

"Dune. I realize your bravado is based on the fear of not being good enough to be here on merit, but as much as I hate to admit it, you *are* here. Stop with the theatrics and dig in to do the job. You could be a great Amberloq if you set aside your insecurities and engage."

He looks at me like I've grown a second head.

"You've been wearing your helmet too tight, frosty. I'm not afraid of anything. I'm the master of my slecking biome and a Biome General. I don't know what you've been smoking but I'm phenomenal."

Why do I even bother being honest with him?

"Suit yourself, but if Honor, Creed, or Keyla's life is on the line, I will know if one of these men is left-handed or has a penchant for knives or tends to bluff when confronted. There's more to being a warrior than how hard you punch and how true your shot is."

"Keep telling yourself that."

I shake my head. "Why are you being such an asshole tonight?"

Before he has a chance to answer, the sound of Honor's footsteps precedes her down the corridor. I slide my tablet back into the thigh pocket of my fatigues and rise as she enters the room. "Princess. How are you?"

"Tired actually. Did everyone else go to bed?"

"Everyone except Lukas. He went to meet Rhylan and Hawk in the security office and asked that we ensure your safe return to the suite when you finished with your visit with Shadow."

Her smile sends a rush of blood through my pounding heart. "It's sweet of him to worry and sweet of you to comply but I've lived in this castle my entire life. I am capable of getting from the King's Tower to the heirs' suite without an escort."

I climb the two stairs that lead out of the great room and join her in the main corridor. "All due respect, Princess. That was before a faction within the citizenship targeted you for elimination. For now, we will take no chances with your life. You are ours to protect."

She presses a gentle hand against my jaw and smiles. "For now, I'll accept that. Once we get control of things, though, I won't be treated like a treasure to guard. When I'm at full strength I will be your leader and a warrior to be reckoned with."

"I have no doubt it is just a matter of days." I gesture toward the door. "After you, Princess."

Dune

Tundra is such a kiss-ass. It must be exhausting bending over to lick everyone's boots. He leads the way out of the king's suite and Honor and I follow. I pause at the door to ensure the lock is engaged and then nod to the two guards standing watch. All is secure.

See, I know my job and I do it well.

I don't need to pump myself up to shine in the eyes of everyone around me. I'm good as I am.

And I'll be even better when we get back to the suite and get naked with Honor.

Honestly, other than the adrenaline high of battle and impending danger, the main advantage to being a General of the Crown is inheriting the right to share a suite and bed with Honor Thornebane.

I thought after the four of us messed around we'd be doing that more often.

Not so far.

Still, there is a little night left. If Tundra and I get her back to the suite and have a chance to have her to ourselves for a sexy session, we'll make an impression. The Iceman might be a by-the-book stick in the mud in all things, but he's a phenom with the bump and grind.

Not that I'd tell him that.

The three of us walk the polished floors of the castle and arrive back to the guarded corridor that leads to the heirs' suite without incident.

"Good evening, gentlemen. Thank you." Honor steps through the doorway when they open the doors, Tundra at her side and me covering her back.

I can't complain about being the guy on her six.

Honor has a great ass.

At the end of the hall, Tundra disengages the security protocols and opens the door to the suite.

Home at last.

"That was a long one." I sit on the low bench inside the door and bend to untie my combat boots. "What do you say, folks, straight to bed?"

Honor stretches. "I'm looking forward to it, but first, I'd like a warm bath."

"A perfect way to unwind after a stressful day." Tundra sets his boots neatly on the floor of the closet by the door. "Let me run that for you, Princess."

"Thank you, Tundra."

"My pleasure."

"I'm going to fill the kettle and make some peppermint tea. Would either of you like some?"

"I would love some, thank you," Tundra says.

"I'll pass, thanks." I sit on the bench, watching the two of them interacting. They're so slecking domestic.

Tundra strikes off to Honor's suite to start her bath and Honor goes to the kitchen to make their tea. Am I the only one getting hives from all this? I pictured this scenario with more of a frantic strip to nail her to the wall with her legs wrapped around my hips.

The door opens again, and Lukas is back.

Slecking hell. This night gets better and better.

"Where's Honor and Tundra?"

"If I say getting hot and sweaty in the bathroom, would you leave?"

He barks a laugh. "I'd leave you here pouting and go join them, yeah."

"You're back," Tundra says, exiting Honor's room. "How did things go in the security office?"

"Badly, and I'm too tired to get into it now. What's the plan for the evening?"

"Honor is looking forward to a hot bath and some peppermint tea. Her water is running and she's in the kitchen starting the kettle."

"Sounds perfect. I'll see if I can be of assistance."

Lukas leaves Tundra and me in the living room and strides down the hall toward the kitchen.

"Why did you do that?"

"Do what?" Tundra asks, frowning at me.

"Include him in our evening."

Tundra arches a brow and chuckles. "I told the man that Honor is making tea."

I stand up and throw him a look. "You're pathetic, you know that?"

"And something foul has crawled so far up your ass you don't even realize you're sabotaging your place here. Grow up and leave that chip you carry on your shoulder at the door."

"You grow up," I snap. Granted, that wasn't the most mature comeback I've ever thrown out there, but I'm tired. "And for your information, I don't have a chip on my shoulder."

"Whatever you say, chip."

"You're an asshole."

"Then I guess it takes one to know one."

"Such a slecking kiss-ass."

Tundra walks off and something inside me snaps. I lunge, taking a flying run at him. Before I land my first punch, he spreads his wings, spins back, and catches me in the chest with the spine of his wing.

The hit is like being struck by a quarry truck.

My feet come off the ground as I'm knocked sailing into the air. I crash over the stone coffee table and land hard in a tangled mess of arms, legs, and wings.

Rolling to my feet, I'm ready to launch again when Honor comes running back into the room and glares at the two of us.

"What now?"

Tundra shakes his head. "It's nothing, Princess. When Dune stews about things he gets chippy and is quick to swing. I've been alone with him long enough to read the signs. He came at me. I shut him down. There's no room in this union for hotheads and ill-tempered fools. He hasn't realized that yet."

"Sleck off, Tundra."

Tundra pretends like he doesn't hear me.

"You've had enough excitement for one day, Princess," he says. "Why don't the two of you take your tea into your suite and relax. I've started the water in your tub and added lavender and erindine to soothe your day away. Enjoy."

"What about you two?"

"Dune can take Lukas's room for the night to cool down. And I'll be fine on the sofa."

"Are you sure?"

He winks at her and offers her one of his super sappy smiles. "Positive."

Honor looks from Tundra to me and then exhales. "I honestly don't have the energy tonight to argue. Thank you, Tundra. Good night."

Honor

I leave Tundra and Dune in the living room and head into my bedroom. I ache all over. From my weakened state, to training, to exploring the library at Amberloq Hall, to sitting in a not-so-comfy chair for a two-hour chat session with Shadow. I am done.

Stripping off my clothes, I follow the rush of water into my bathroom and turn off the faucets. The tub is half full but once I'm in there, and hopefully Lukas too, that'll bring the water level up quite a bit.

I test the temperature with a lazy swirl of my fingers through the pink, erindine bubbles. It's a little warm, but that's fine. I need to pee first and get fresh towels out for us anyway.

Once that's taken care of, I lift my foot over the side of the tub and ease into the water. "Perfection."

"I think that was my line," Lukas says, coming in with two mugs of tea. "Do you still want this?"

"Hells yes. Set them on the vanity for a second and then, in that cupboard, there is a tub caddy. Can you grab it for me?"

He does as I ask and secures the caddy in place across the tub and in front of me. Then he brings our tea over. "Would you like solitude or company?"

"Definitely company. I'd like you to get naked and join me for an evening soak."

"I can do that." He sets the teas down, steps into the toilet room for a moment, and then comes back, washes up, and strips down.

Watching Lukas get naked is no hardship. He's a beautiful man—tall, dark, and ruggedly handsome. He's got ribbed abs and strong shoulders that taper to a slim waist and the sexy man 'V' from his hips pointing down to his groin.

"Shall I slow things down and give you longer to ogle or am I good to join you?"

I grin at his teasing. "As tempting as it is to ask for a few runway turns, far be it from me to objectify you."

He chuckles, stepping into the tub at the opposite end so he's facing me. "I don't know. I find being objectified by you sexy. I give you permission to ogle me as much and for as long as you wish."

To emphasize his point, he runs a lazy caress under his sac and his cock thickens, and pulses toward me.

I giggle and point to the water. "First we relax. We'll get to that later."

It takes a moment to get him seated and to figure out where his feet and mine should go to make this work, but we manage. He plants his feet on the bottom of the tub outside my thighs and I rest the bottoms of my feet against his junk and give him a couple of gentle nudges.

"So, how was the security office?" I ask, picking up my tea while still teasing his cock with my toes.

"Terrible, but I've taken the steps that need taking and we will dive into that tomorrow. For right now, let's pretend there is no world beyond this room."

"I like the sound of that. Are you sure it can all wait until tomorrow?"

"I am. And as much as I am loving this, I would tell you if we needed to do something more productive."

I relax against the back of the tub and sip my tea. "Good. Then, tomorrow it is."

"How was your visit with Shadow? His world must be rocked."

"It is. Although the moment we stopped talking about that and shifted the conversation to what's been happening with me and my transition into power, he seemed much better."

"I can see that. He's a man of observation and service. To be the focus of attention and having to be the one expressing his feelings must be jarring for him."

We sip our tea for a few minutes, both of us keeping company with our own thoughts.

"What do you suppose was happening between Dune and Tundra?" I ask. "A lover's spat?"

He shakes his head. "I don't get that vibe from them at all. If I were to guess, I'd say they are the furthest thing from lovers. They are antagonists who take out their frustrations with sex."

"That sounds rather hollow."

"If they were the kind of men looking for a warm and fuzzy relationship, it would be hollow. They aren't... or at least haven't been up until now."

"So, what do you think that scuffle was about?"

Lukas swallows and lowers his cup from his lips. "Likely,

exactly what Tundra said. Dune got chippy and tried to start something and he shut it down."

It's not hard to imagine that scenario.

"What's your read on Dune?"

Lukas shrugs. "My first impression is that he's one helluva fighter but shit at being around people. Maybe that's ego or anxiety or some deep dark desire to keep from letting people too close. I'm not sure. The point is, he's been placed in our lives and those kinks will have to get ironed out or Tundra won't be the only one knocking him on his ass."

That was pretty much my take on him too.

"Do you think it would be too invasive for me to take a stroll through his dream plane and see what's going on in his subconscious mind?"

Lukas chuckles. "You can do that?"

I waggle my brow and grin. "Mind guardian fae can do lots of mind-bendy tricks."

He tilts his head and seems to consider that. "No. In his current state of aggression, I think he'd take your presence in his mind as an invasion of privacy."

He's probably right. Although, I'm very curious to peel back the layers and see the real Dune underneath. He sets his mug back onto the bridge across the tub and lifts one of my feet to massage the sole.

Ohmygods it feels so good.

"Is that how we shared that first orgasm session?"

I think about the two of us lying in opposite ends of the suite and how it felt to get off with him in my head.

My nipples tighten and send a zing of hunger down to my core. "No. That wasn't the dream plane. That was just my mind guardian gifts out of control."

"Mmm... I like you out of control."

I close my eyes and soak in the pressure of his fingers working the tension out of my foot. When he gives a pinch and twist between my toes, I can't help but groan. "Oh... where'd you learn to do that?"

"I dated a massage therapist for a few months and picked up a few things."

"Mhmm... I remember." He gave me a back massage a week or two ago and had me orgasming simply by the way he rubbed my spinal ridges.

By the heated look he gives me, he remembers too.

I finish my tea and set it on the tray. That's when I notice his mug isn't empty. "Didn't you like your tea?"

"I'm English. I loved it. I'm simply thirsty for something else now."

Heat blooms deep in my belly and I swallow. "Shall we get rid of this tray?"

He leans forward and the tub caddy is disconnected and set on the bathroom floor without preamble. "Now what, Princess? What are you in the mood for?"

I push up in the water and make like a horny mermaid and meet him chest-to-chest. He cups my jaw in his hands and pulls me in for a kiss.

Lukas is a warrior in all things. He is confident, assertive, and there is never any hesitation. When he wants something, he goes for it.

And, right now, he wants my mouth.

His lips move over mine with a possession that should frighten me. It doesn't... but it should.

He wants to do more than to kiss me.

He wants to consume me.

I meet his heightened aggression, sweep my tongue into his mouth, and groan as my body awakens to every possibility. Splitting my legs, I straddle his hips.

Water splashes out of the tub, but I don't care. Short of flooding the floor below us, I don't care how choppy the waters are.

He has to sit up for my thighs to fit around his waist, but we make it work.

Breaking the kiss, he shifts his hold to grab my shoulders from behind. Tipping me backward, he claims my breast. A nip to the hardened peak sends a rush of sensation through me and I gasp.

The gentle swirl of his tongue to soothe the ache follows. I'm lost... Warm water splashes up my ribs. Our bodies move with an easy glide and slide. His touch is a claim as he takes without apology and yet gives me so much in return.

His hand leaves my flesh and he flicks his fingers through the air. The lights turn off and we're plunged into sensory overload. A moment later, a gentle glow warms the darkness and it's like he lit a dozen candles.

Only I don't have candles in here.

I'm about to ask him how he did that when he lifts my hips and props the head of his erection at my entrance. Some asinine rule about sex in a bubble bath not being good for you flashes through my mind but there's no way I'm bringing that up.

Stopping the sex would be worse.

With his grip firmly on my upper thighs, he guides me down his shaft and we both exhale as I take him in fully. "Fuck. I needed this," he growls.

"It's nice to be needed."

There isn't a lot of room for movement in here, but when his hands shift up the ridges of my ribs and start to lift and then impale me again, I get the picture.

Gripping the smooth, enamel of the tub edge with each hand, I rise on my knees a little and then take him once... twice... over and over.

Water rocks and splashes between us, but I don't care. The rise and fall of heat against my flesh only enriches my body's response.

"That's it," Lukas says, his voice rough. "Ride me hard. I feel your insides clenching—squeezing me."

I feel it too.

The rub of him filling me is delicious and I could do this forever and be breathless and replete but it won't get me where I want to go. To orgasm— "I need more."

"Then more you shall have." The lusty edge to his voice is almost enough.

I'm close. Oh, gods, so close to breaking apart and gripping hold of him.

Both of his hands cup my breasts and as his thumbs roll over the peaks of my nipples something wholly magical snaps against my skin.

The current of sexual energy zings straight from the nerve endings of my boobs straight to my core.

"Oh, gods, what did you do?"

"You like?"

My mind is spinning. It felt wild and amazing and a little out of control. I almost can't decide if I loved it or if it was too much.

"That was just a taste. Do you want more?"

My heart is racing at the thought. I'll lose my grip, I know I will. I meet his gaze in the soft glow. There is only him and I and then the rest of the world recedes in shadow.

"I want more," I breathe, only half sure I'll survive. "I want more than a taste. I want to devour everything you give me."

Something shifts in his gaze and his mental energy fritzes for a second. "Fuck. When you lose it, I'll be right behind you."

I close my eyes, focusing on the glorious rub of him against my insides, his mouth against my neck... my collarbone... my shoulder...

Another surge of magic hits and my body lights up.

But he doesn't stop.

This surge of his power hits my aching core and my mind

shatters. The orgasm building inside me detonates and I arch back and close my eyes.

I cry out and have no idea if I'm calling his name or cursing or singing my favorite song.

There's no making sense of my world.

And still, he doesn't stop.

He grips the top of my thighs and pins me against his hips, grunting as his release hits too. With his head thrown back and his face twisted in panting breaths, he is the vision of violent ecstasy.

I did that to him.

I've had many lovers, some of them exceptional, but not one of them ever looked like their soul was breaking apart as they spilled into me.

And just like that, my English military man steals another piece of my heart. This strong, deadly, incredibly worldly man finds completion inside me.

"Thank you," I whisper, falling forward to kiss his late-night, stubbled jaw as he catches his breath. His heart pounds against my palm and I'm pleased with myself. "That was incredible."

His arms come around me and he pulls me to lay against his chest. "*You* are incredible. Now, let's get you dried off. I think I have some heavy-duty maintenance work to do before we flood the people downstairs and they come to investigate."

I sit up wide-eyed. "Do you think they will?"

He laughs. "Of course, they will. That's why we need to throw down some towels."

I rise on my knees, the intensity of the moment broken but the magic still very much alive. Looking over the side of the tub I burst out laughing. "Oh, shit. I don't know if there are enough towels in the castle to soak up all that water. Houston, we have a problem."

CHAPTER FOUR

Tundra

I wake early and make myself useful in the kitchen. Prior to being exiled to Mount Nekko to reflect on my behavior, I hadn't been much of a cook. Funny what a couple of years on a mountaintop can teach you. If only Dune had learned half as much.

I start the coffee and pull out enough peppers, mushrooms, and eggs to make us omelets.

Where I took the opportunity to read and expand my understanding of philosophy, history, and psychology, Dune chose to practice offensive skills.

When I meditated and worked on self-awareness, he chose to practice offensive skills.

And when our loneliness and desperation finally took us over and we succumbed to the need to be sexual... he chose to practice offensive skills.

He may not have drawn knives and tried to stab me when we were together, but he never allowed me to see his true self. So guarded. So hostile.

I probably know him better than anyone else alive and yet I don't know him at all.

"Good morning." Lukas shuffles in looking scruffy and wearing his boxers. "Oh, you started the coffee. Bless you."

"Just. It's not ready." I pull down four mugs and set them on the island countertop. "A good night?"

I don't mean to pry but I admit, after hearing him and Honor from behind the closed door for several rounds of orgasms last night, I'd like to share in a bit of the afterglow.

Lukas reaches into the fridge to retrieve the cream and his mouth quirks up at the side. "A great night, actually. Sorry if we disturbed you. I threw up a veil of privacy but that wasn't until halfway into our night."

"Halfway? Good gods, man. You need more than coffee. I thought you two completed a marathon and now I learn that was only *half* the night?"

He chuckles and pours cream into his empty mug. "It's too easy to get carried away with her. She's spectacular."

"You love her."

Lukas meets my gaze and there's no way he can deny it. It's written all over his face. "More with every breath I take."

Good. That's good. "The two of you wear it well. She deserves that kind of devotion."

The coffee machine stops humming and I pour us each a cup.

"She thinks highly of you, too."

I blow across the rim of my mug and take that to heart. "Like you said. She's spectacular."

"Are my ears burning or do I need to pull out my weapons? I hope the *she* in that statement is yours truly." Honor joins us, her long hair messy and out of place. Her thighs are bare under the t-shirt Lukas wore last night, and her smile is radiant.

I straighten and lower my chin. "She most definitely is you,

Princess. Lukas and I were taking a moment to count our blessings. We are both thankful to be included in your life."

Her amethyst eyes practically glow with warmth and affection. "And I'm thankful for you both as well. Will you pour me a mug, please?"

While I comply and get her set up with a coffee, she bends over to smell the freshly cut peppers. The shift in position lifts the hem of Lukas's t-shirt, and with her back toward me, I'm rewarded with a glorious view of a lacy thong disappearing between the rounds of the most perfect ass I've ever seen.

My body responds unbidden.

Lukas catches me looking and I flash him an apologetic glance before I give them my back and focus on assembling the ingredients for our breakfast. "I was looking through the files loaded into the Amberloq security library and realized we have a great deal of ground to cover this morning. I took the liberty of starting breakfast."

"That's sweet of you, Tundra. Thank you."

Yes. Sweet. That's the word she uses with me more often than any other. While it's not a bad thing, I am so much more. I just long for the chance to show her.

"I used to have a container of dried peppers from the castle garden up in this cabinet. They would be perfect for eggs, if you're game to try them." Honor swings open the cabinet door to search the shelves. "Creed hated the taste, so I bet they're still here."

She's on her toes reaching for the top shelf. My first instinct is to rush over and help her but yeah, there's that sweet ass of hers again.

"Kind of makes you want to move everything to the top shelves, doesn't it?" Lukas says.

I adjust my pants, the pressure behind my fly getting restrictive.

Honor turns around looking curious. "Why is that?"

"Because we're both checking out your ass and getting hard doing it."

Honor looks from him to me and blushes. "Sorry. I didn't mean to flash you or make things weird."

I swallow. "There's nothing weird. No harm done."

Lukas chuckles. "No harm, no, but something definitely shifted in your pants. You doing all right over there, Iceman?"

When Dune calls me that, it's meant as a slur. I don't get the same impression from Lukas. In fact, unless I'm misreading things completely, I think he's flirting with me. "As you said earlier. It's too easy to get carried away with her."

Honor looks at him and smiles. "You say the sweetest things when I'm not in the room. It almost makes me want to leave so the two of you can talk about me some more."

Lukas chuckles. "Or you could stay and we could help Tundra with a problem he's having."

"Oh, even better. What's the matter? How can we help?"

My cheeks flush hot and I meet Lukas's teasing gaze. "There's no problem, Princess. All is well."

"Oh, let's make a new rule," Lukas says, enjoying this much too much. "No lies between us. If we're going to do this. If we're to make lasting bonds, we need to be upfront and honest."

"Exactly." Honor extends her hand into the air between us. "I give you both my word."

Lukas sets his hand on hers and grins. "I do as well. How 'bout it, T? You game for full transparency?"

I roll my eyes, seeing where he's going with this and realizing there is no way to not take this oath. "Only the truth shall be shared between us. I do so swear."

Honor beams. "Excellent. So, now do I get to unwrap my present?"

I shrug. "I'm not sure what you mean? Present?"

Honor places her palm against the front of my pants and gently grinds my cock. "Isn't this meant for me?"

The breath rushes from my lungs and I'm not sure whether to be embarrassed and retreat or stand my ground and take their teasing. "I'm sorry. I didn't mean to—"

Honor's mouth claims mine and ends any explanation I was attempting to piece together. Between one thought and another, my mind is wiped of all reason. Her tongue sweeps the seam of my lips as her hands wrap around my back and crush us together.

Sweet mercies she's delicious. Her mouth tastes like the mint of her toothpaste, but that's not what I mean. She's confident and driven by a code and her skin is as soft to touch as the finest silk.

Pressed against her as we are, there's nothing I want more than to shift my hand under her t-shirt and cup the lush rounds of her breasts.

But this is her advance on me, not the other way around. She gets to decide where this goes. I just hope it's going where I think it is because I long for her. After hearing her feminine cries of release last night, I need to be more to her than her sweet bodyguard.

Distracted as I am, I miss when she frees the buttons of my pants from their moorings. I don't, however, miss my pants pool to my ankles.

The weighty *flump* of them hitting the tiles accompanies a rush of cool air against my hot skin. And then she's got her hands in the waistband of my underwear and is stretching them to clear the crown of my cock.

"See. I knew you had a present for me." She bends to shove my boxers down my thighs and then—

"Oh, sweet powers." I pike, gripping the edge of the countertop as her mouth parts over my stiff cock. My heart is pounding in my chest as I fight not to pass out from the massive surge of blood flow rushing to her location.

"She's got skills, doesn't she?"

I barely register Lukas's question but manage to focus enough to find him sitting at the little table in the corner. He's tugged his boxers down and is stroking himself while watching us.

Honor slides her mouth up my shaft until I swear there's no possible way she can take any more. Then she glides back to the tip where she pauses and flicks her tongue through my slit.

I glance down and it's the most beautiful sight I've ever seen. Her eyes are closed and there's a heavenly smile on her face, her cheeks hollowed as she sucks me off. She's resplendent.

The burn at the base of my sac bears down on me and my eyes roll back into my head.

"You doing all right there, T?" Lukas says. "Don't go off yet, my brother. Our girl can do that for ages. Soak it in."

I chuff. "Trust me. Soaking it all in is exactly why I'm about to go off early."

Honor chuckles and the vibration of her amusement tingles over my flesh. I shudder and draw a deep breath. "Slecking hell, you're beautiful."

My reward for that is her teeth scoring my shaft as she swallows me down once more.

"Oh, and you bite."

Lukas barks a laugh. "Yes, she does. I forgot to warn you about that."

I force my eyes open and take in the slow and steady stroke Lukas is using on his own stiff cock. "Do you like watching us?"

Lukas grins. "I do. And I figure it's only fair since you were listening to us last night and probably did the same thing. How many times did you stroke yourself off and come with us last night?"

I shake my head, casting a look up to the ceiling. "This oath of perfect honesty is going to bite me in the ass, isn't it?"

Lukas laughs. "Maybe. How many times, T?"

"Three."

Lukas

"Three." I enjoy the flush of his cheeks more than I probably should. "Sorry about that. We should've opened the door and invited you in."

"It's fine," he says, his voice breathy.

He's holding back. I can see his apprehension and realize his manners are getting in the way. "Don't worry about being polite with her. Honor is in this with us and is a very aggressive lover. Be yourself. It'll make things so much hotter for all of us. Oh, and don't worry about coming in her mouth. She loves it. She's dying to suck you dry, aren't you, babe?"

"Mhmm..."

His eyes roll closed and he laces the fingers of his free hand into her long, silver hair. The fingers of his other hand have gone white from gripping the countertop as if his life depended on him not losing his hold.

Yeah, I know how he feels. Honor gives great head.

A surge of sexual energy rushes down my spine and straight to my cock. Over the past six months, I've been on the outside of the door with the quint enough times to understand where he was last night.

It's *waaay* better to be on the inside.

Watching her practically stops my heart. She's incredibly beautiful when she is fully engaged. I don't know if she's always been aggressive or if it's something she picked up during the decade of altered time in the Human Realm, but she certainly doesn't act like a princess behind closed doors.

"Having fun, Princess?"

"Mhmm," she mumbles around Tundra's cock.

"How about you, big guy? Are you having fun?"

Tundra's eyes are pinched shut, his breathing coming in

heady bursts. His hand is caressing the back of Honor's head as his hips gently sway to thrust in and out of her mouth. He's lost in the sensation and about to lose his load.

"So, fucking hot."

And he is. Insanely tall with pale skin, ebony hair, and white-feathered wings that when folded closed rise above his head and taper to below his muscled calves. His plumage is that of a snowy owl and he's just as majestic and graceful in flight.

He's a solid guy.

Smart. Considerate. And dedicated.

"This is just a morning wake-up session before a long day," I say, picking up my pace with my palm. "The next chance we get, you and I have familiarizing to do with one another."

Tundra's eyes flip open and he meets my gaze.

So hot…

With our gaze locked, I go all-in on pumping myself off. It doesn't take me long to start panting, the burn of my release pushing hard at the base of my cock.

The *click, click, click* of precum beats off my jackhammer rhythm. Tundra is as invested in my actions as I am and, if I'm reading him right, if he wasn't pinned in place and getting swallowed down, he'd be over here sucking me off.

The mental image of that trips my defenses and my muscles seize. Tundra curses and starts to pump his hips. The two of us fill the air with throaty cries of release, all the while watching the other shatter.

It's intense. It's intimate. It's insanely hot.

My heart hammers in my chest as I arch back in my chair and close my eyes. The image of Tundra is seared into my vision as warm streams of cum spill onto my navel and over my hand.

It's hard to believe I've even got anything left in me after last night, but yeah, I'm inspired. Eventually, though, the world slows its spin and my muscles ease and the kitchen falls still.

"Thank you, boys," Honor says. "I think the breathy pants of two spent men mark the breakfast sampler as a solid success." I open up my eyes and meet Honor's smile as she hands me a damp cloth.

"I think you're right, babe."

Tundra is doubled over the countertop, his head resting against his forearms.

"You okay, big guy?" I take care of the worst of the mess and then stand to run the cloth under the faucet. The trip to the sink takes me over to where Tundra is still taking a time out. "Seriously, man. You good?"

He lifts his head and I get it.

"Yeah. It was intense."

He straightens, turns, and without saying a word, he claims my mouth. The kiss is heated but not in the 'let's get something going' kind of way. No. This kiss is all about acknowledging a searing connection.

I felt it too.

I meet his lips with the answer to his unspoken question. Yes, I'm right there with you.

After a moment of exploration, he slows the kiss and eases back. "Does this mean you've forgiven me for our first meeting?"

I grin. "You mean when I shot you?"

He chuckles and steps back. "You mean when you emptied your pea-shooter at me?"

I let him have that. My bullets had no effect on slowing him down. In my defense, I didn't know about Elbirfae and their natural shielding.

I rinse the cloth Honor gave me, finish washing up, and hand it to Tundra so he can do the same. "This was fun. Let's get back to this soon."

"I look forward to it." He wipes himself before pulling up his pants and then gathers Honor in his arms. When he hugs her, he brings his wings around and cages her completely against his body. "Thank you. That was an unexpected gift. I'm sorry if I was aggressive with you at the end."

Honor laughs and tips her face up to kiss him. "I'm not the fragile kind of princess. I'm a warrior out in the world and in the bedroom. Don't ever be afraid you're hurting me. I won't let you."

"Fair enough."

With that settled, the three of us look around the kitchen and go back to starting our day.

CHAPTER FIVE

Dune

$\mathcal{I}$'m not sure what I missed last night but the dynamic between Tundra, Lukas, and our princess has changed. I don't think he joined them in Honor's suite because I took a stroll to the kitchen in the middle of the night and he was snoring on one of the couches.

Still, something is different.

The four of us came down to the security center at the crack of nine this morning, which they said was late but I consider early. Tundra shoved a plate into my hand and told me to eat it in transit or miss the start of Lukas's briefing.

There's no way I'm getting left behind on anything Lukas is in charge of, so I wolfed down the omelet and here we are.

"Do you honestly think Breard has any grounds to oust Creed?" Honor asks, looking pissed.

Rhylan calls up the next screen of legalese and shakes his head. "I don't, but I'm not an expert. So far, those who know better than me are saying they highly doubt it."

"But we don't want to get caught unprepared," Lukas says. "If we anticipate the worst coming at us, we can prepare and hopefully derail their attempts."

"They can go fuck themselves," Creed snaps. "There's no way I'll hand this quadrant over to Ruic Breard or any other titan of ambition who wants the cream to rise above the citizenship. I rule the way Thornebane's have always ruled—for the people."

Honor crosses her arms and stares up at the profile information hovering above the table. "What else do you think they'll throw at us?"

Lukas and Rhylan go on to list all the ways we came up with last night of how we think Ruic will try to screw us over. Currency. Violence. Non-confidence. Slander.

"One thing is for sure," Tundra says, tapping off the screen of his tablet, "our current Amberloq force isn't up to fighting off an army if they attack."

"Even with the Thornebane Quad and the Phoenix Quint behind you," Rhylan adds.

Creed chuckles. "The Thornebane Quad? Is that what they're calling us now?"

Rhylan grins. "I think it's damn catchy."

"My point is we need more Amberloq behind us," Tundra says.

Look at him getting all assertive with the group. Yeah, definitely something changed.

"You're right, T," Lukas says. "And while Hawk and I take yet another run at Hunter and the goblin we arrested, you guys start formulating a plan on how to rally more soldiers for the Amberloq army."

"I still want to know where my general is for the Forested Jungle Biome," Honor says.

Lukas chuckles. "Looking to expand our numbers, babe? Are we falling down on the job?"

She rolls her eyes. "No. Just our Amberloq numbers, but who

knows. Since Thornebane Quad is already taken, maybe a Thornebane Quint isn't such a bad idea."

Hawk barks a laugh and slaps a hand on Lukas's shoulder. "I probably shouldn't find this as funny as I do, but yeah... I totally do."

Lukas shrugs off the hold and points toward the exit. "Lead the way, Barron. We've got traitors to break. You can mock me later."

"Don't kid yourself. I will."

"So, what's your plan for the interrogation of the prisoners," Rhylan asks.

Hawk grins. "We'll smash Hunter into tiny bits and send him back to his traitor wife broken and bleeding."

That's messed up. "Isn't that your brother?"

Hawk meets my gaze and smiles. "Half brother. Feel free to think of us as high-achievers in dysfunction."

The two of them leave and Honor closes in. "That leaves the five of us to come up with an Amberloq army in the next days and months. Where should we start?"

It's Rhylan who speaks up first. "I've been thinking about that. If I might make a suggestion...?"

He pauses and genuinely seems to be giving Honor the choice of whether or not he can contribute to the conversation.

She shrugs. "Go ahead."

"The enlistment age for the Amberloq trials has always been twenty-one or the species equivalent. You could petition the king to approve an exception until your numbers bolster. I suggest dropping it to nineteen and holding the trials right here on the castle grounds. That way, the prospects can experience what they're fighting for."

Honor looks at Tundra and me. "What do you think about an age drop? Would you have been ready to commit to the Amberloq earlier?"

Tundra looks at me and we both nod. "I knew from the time I was an adolescent," I say.

"You're still an adolescent," Tundra says.

I'm about to lash out when I realize he's joking. "My point is that those of us who grow up dreaming of joining the Amberloq start dreaming at a young age."

"For Elbirfae, maybe," Rhylan says. "If I thought I could've been Amberloq, I would've been lined up at the trials waiting to sign up, but everyone knows it's the Elbirfae who get inducted and who get the prime posts. If, by some miracle, a wizard or an earth fae or a giant were accepted, they'd get sent to the outposts in the fringe."

Honor scowls and looks like she's about to argue when Tundra stops her. "He's not wrong, Princess. Your aunt strongly preferred Elbirfae in her army over the other species."

"What? Why?"

"Because we're better," I say before my brain catches up with my tongue.

Cue the daggered glares stabbing me until I'm writhing on the ground. "What I mean is that in battle, Elbirfae have strength and the ability to fly—"

"So do dragons," Rhylan says. "Not to mention pixies and wind sprites and sky gnomes."

"Pixies aren't strong."

Rhylan laughs. "You've obviously never fought one while he or she is in a rage. Don't underestimate them merely because of their size."

"Fine, Elbirfae also have natural armor."

"Again, so do dragons and stone giants and some species of haunts."

He can't be serious. "Do you really want a haunt guarding the royal couple? They consume the lives of fae and take over."

Rhylan shrugs. "We were talking about abilities. Not all

haunts are dark, and yes, I can think of situations when having a haunt on the payroll could be an asset."

"That's delusional."

"No, it's not," Honor says. "I agree with Rhylan. Being exclusionary creates division. Amberloq should be held to the highest standards and be the best people for the job regardless of species or size or presumed alliances. We can do better."

I scrub a hand over my face and gesture for Tundra to join the conversation. "Tell them. The reason Elbirfae dominate the crown forces is that we are the best suited for the job."

Tundra frowns. "I agree we are ideally suited for the job but not necessarily the best suited. Look at how easily Calli handled herself against the missile attack. She flies. She fights. And she grows hot enough that it's like she's wearing armor. If someone like her wanted to be on our team, I wouldn't turn her away."

"But that's not how it's done."

"That's not how Valorous did it," Honor says. "Rhylan is right. I say we re-evaluate past practices and welcome all species and all races to join the trials. And yes, drop the applicant age to nineteen temporarily. We'll need crown approval, of course."

"Granted," Creed says.

Honor smiles. "See how easily things work when the two most powerful Thornebanes are working as a team?"

I sigh and throw up my hands.

I don't know why they look so pleased. Being an Amberloq is an exclusive honor. Opening the doors will ruin everything that is special about it.

Honor

Whatever is bugging Dune, has seriously shoved a spur up his ass. As my Desert Biome General stomps off to get some air, I continue the conversation I'm having with Creed, Rhylan, and Tundra. "So, we'll announce a trials competition as soon as we have the details figured out and ensure everyone feels welcome. We'll also lower the age of qualification. What else?"

"I think we need to travel to the Forested Jungle Biome and assess what happened there," Tundra says.

Creed nods. "Agreed. I find it alarming that no representative has answered the call."

Rhylan finishes typing something on his tablet and then gives us his full attention. "I think the two of you should address the quadrant to discuss the importance of the Amberloq. That will give Creed a chance to get in front of the citizens to speak about the changes you're implementing and maybe head off some of the criticisms we anticipate coming your way."

That's a good idea.

As much as I want to disagree with and hate everything Rhylan says on principle, he's really helpful. He seems to truly care and support my brother.

Yes, I know, Lukas, Calli, and Creed tried to get me to see how Laryssa put him in an untenable situation.

I'm starting to see that now.

I don't forgive him for capturing me time and again and bringing me back to Laryssa's prison, but I admit, he never mistreated me or abused his power or my situation like some of the other guards.

"On a more sensitive note," Tundra says, raising a finger. "May I make another suggestion, King Creed?"

Creed grows serious but doesn't seem guarded in any way. "Of course, Tundra. That's why we're here. What's on your mind."

"I mean you no disrespect, sire, but might I suggest you mask the effects of the Blood Witch's curse until Lukas has removed it? While we all understand you are no longer under her thrall, I believe your eyes are found to be unnerving to the citizens."

"That's not his fault," Rhylan snaps.

"No. Of course, it's not. My thought is simply that if Ruic Breard wants to create a disconnect between King Creed and the citizens of Dornte, having him display evidence of his past difficulties might not instill confidence in those who might be swayed."

Creed raises his hand to stop whatever Rhylan is about to say in my brother's defense. "It's fine, Rhy. He's not wrong and we all know it. I don't like looking in the mirror and seeing these soulless black holes staring back at me. It can't be any different for anyone else."

"Lukas is confident he can remove the curse," I say. "We've talked about it several times. It's just a matter of finding a time when neither you or he are racing around putting out fires."

Creed nods. "I understand that but maybe we need to make time and let the realm wait for a bit. I admit, I want to be rid of this mindless beast prowling around inside me. Without a master, I'm worried there won't be anyone to control it if it ever breaks free."

Rhylan frowns and squeezes Creed's shoulder. "We've got you no matter what happens."

Creed winks at the dragon and then returns his attention to the conversation. "In the meantime, I'll speak to Keyla about what to do to minimize the impact of what I've been left with."

"Have Hawk or Keyla look into purple contact lenses from the Human Realm," I suggest. "Changing eye color is something they do all the time for fun, for costumes, and transformations in movies."

Rhylan's dragon growls. "He shouldn't need to lie and conceal himself. He's not at fault for what was done to him by those bitches."

"It's fine, Rhy." Creed slides a hand along Rhylan's jaw and steps close. "They're right. Until the curse is dealt with, we have to change the optics. Thank you for standing as my champion, but I don't need defending. I agree with them."

A private look passes between them and I block the mental energy as they speak to one another telepathically. Even with me giving them privacy, I can't help but be affected by the depth of affection they share.

When the moment ends, I'm more than ready to move on and move out. "Give Dune, Tundra, and I the day to come up with details on the trials and then we'll present our plans. If you approve, we'll address the citizens tomorrow afternoon. I want a chance to look through the Chronicles of the Amberloq and see how the past Guardians handled the trials."

"That's a solid plan. You three do that and we'll work with Keyla about what message we want to send to the citizens to ward off Ruic's criticisms."

I lean in and hug my brother. "Perfect. We'll meet up later and compare ideas."

The three of us leave the security office and I pause in the corridor. "Tundra, will you please go to the prisoner suites and wait for Lukas to finish with the interrogations? I want to go to Amberloq Hall for a few hours. If the two of you can meet Dune and me there later, that would be great."

"Of course, Princess. Be safe." Tundra turns his gaze to Dune and frowns. "Be alert."

Dune and I stand there watching Tundra stride off down the hall. Damn, those wings of his are spectacular. Downy soft and snow white with tiny black flecks here and there for patterning. The only downside is that they hide his ass.

Tundra has a great ass.

Images of our breakfast fun fill my mind and I fight not to groan. I loved everything about sucking Tundra off in the kitchen this morning—the soft skin shifting over his solid shaft, the grip of his hand in my hair as he got more aggressive at the end, and the unique sweetness of Elbirfae cum.

The only problem is that it wasn't enough. Tundra is a strong warrior with a sweet soul, but I sense so much more beneath the surface. He has passion he's holding back, and I want to free it and truly know him.

A not-so-subtle sigh lets off beside me and I catch the roll of Dune's eyes. How could two men who spent so much time together be so different? Dune is so distant and flippant, I'm not even sure he's aware of it.

I point into the open doorway of the empty training center. "You and I are going to have a much-needed private chat. After you."

I follow him inside and close the door. "Whatever it is, I'm done. Get it off your chest. I won't have drama on my team and right now, you're oozing hostility and frustration. What's wrong?"

Dune shrugs and frowns at me like a petulant child.

"I'm serious, Dune. You've got a problem and we're not leaving here until you spit it out and have your say."

"That's not how this works. You're the Guardian. I do what you say. Valorous had well-defined lines that none of us crossed. I know my place."

"Apparently you don't because you haven't noticed that I'm not my aunt."

"I've noticed."

By the tone of his voice, I don't think that's a good thing in his mind. "Take a seat." I point to the weight bench. "We'll stay in here all day if we have to, but neither of us leaves until the air is clear."

"That's not necessary."

"I disagree. And like you just pointed out, I'm the Guardian and you're my General."

I grab a wooden chair from beside the door and spin it to

straddle the seat and face him. Crossing my arms over the back of the chair, I rest my chin and wait.

And wait...

And wait some more.

One of the truly important life lessons I learned in the Human Realm is the power of a staring contest. Most people feel the need to fill empty and awkward silences.

I don't.

I can do this all day.

After about five minutes of Dune glaring, he huffs and starts to squirm. "Are we seriously going to waste our morning sitting in here?"

"If you refuse to tell me what's going on, yeah. And in that case, I would argue it's *you* who's wasting our morning sitting here."

He rolls his eyes and my temper flares. "You see, that's what I'm talking about. If you roll your eyes at me once more, I'm going to clock you. I mean it. It's rude, it's disrespectful, and it's maddening."

"You sound like Tundra."

"I'll take that as a compliment."

"It wasn't meant as one."

"Oh, I'm aware. What you don't seem to understand is that Tundra is an exceptional man and he's earning respect and his place at my side."

"Uh-huh."

"What? You don't agree?"

He shrugs.

"No. If you have something to say, say it. No fault. No foul. Right here and right now you've got a free pass to say whatever is on your mind without the threat of repercussion."

Dune chuckles. "I'll pass."

"No, you won't. If you don't speak up, we'll be pulling out the mats and sleeping here tonight. You might have a chip on your shoulder, but I can out stubborn you any day of the week."

Dune meets my gaze and studies my conviction. He doesn't seem to like what he sees. "Can't we forget it?"

"Nope."

He rolls his eyes and I'm off my chair and backhanding him to the floor before I even register my intention to do it. My strike is swift and meets no resistance. "Stop being a petulant prick. Enough with the eye-rolling."

Damnit. Sure, I warned him I would clock him but I hadn't really intended on hitting him. That's not the kind of relationship I want with him.

I shake out my hand and gain some distance.

He tests his split lip and pushes off the ground to reclaim his seat on the bench. "Feel better?"

"Not particularly."

"Strange, most people enjoy punching me."

I sigh. "I'm not most people. I don't want conflict between us. I want to know what I'm doing that is so awful you can't contain your insubordination. Do you not want to be here? Not want to be a General? What is it?"

"I told you, it's nothing. There is no issue."

"Is it me? Do you dislike me? Or is it an authority thing? Or is it a misogynistic thing? Give me a starting point and we'll start to work on things."

"You're never going to let this go, are you?"

"No. I have an Amberloq force of two, Dune. I can't afford to have you hate me. If I've done something, tell me so I can fix it."

"It's not a *you* thing, it's a *me* thing."

All right. Not where I thought this would go.

He launches to his feet and paces toward the treadmills. "Being an Amberloq warrior isn't supposed to be for everyone. It's a selective position. Only the elite should represent and protect the crown. I wasn't a warrior when Valorous distanced herself from your father, so I can't speak about how it was back then, but when the Amberloq were strong and fierce, it was a community to be revered and feared."

"What does that have to do with you being a jerk?"

"Because I was already pegged as a disappointment and a screw-up before Valorous was killed. That was when I had hundreds of soldiers to use as cover. Now there's just me and Tundra. There's no way you and your boyfriend won't realize the universe got it wrong by making me a general. Tundra knows it. He throws it in my face every damned day."

"That's not the impression I get from him at all."

"Then you haven't been listening."

I step back over to my chair and turn it to face him as he works off his anxiety. "Or maybe you're hearing what you're projecting. The only thing I've ever gotten from you and Tundra bickering is that he believes you're better than you're acting and he wants you to take this seriously and smarten up."

"I do take this seriously. Being an Amberloq is all I ever wanted and in my region I was exceptional. I went to those trials confident that I was exactly what the crown needed."

"So, what changed?"

"The trials were harder than I expected and as good as I was in the training squads in the desert, I barely made it when it came to qualifications."

"But you *did* make it."

"Yes, but if you open up recruitment to include dragons and elves and giants, how am I supposed to measure up? What good is it if new recruits are better than a Biome General? You're going to regret having me here. Tundra's right. You deserve better."

I hear the longing in his voice, and I feel for him. "I think when Tundra tells you that this warrior force deserves better, he's saying we deserve better *from* you, not better *than* you."

"We'll agree to disagree on that."

"Okay then, what do you think your greatest strength is as a warrior and, conversely, what is your greatest weakness?"

He rubs his palms against the thighs of his tactical pants and sighs. "I'm a damned good shot and excel in one-on-one combat. I'd feel confident going up against anyone on those terms."

"And your weakness?"

"Everything else is pretty much a wash. Tactical. Teamwork. Following orders. Weapons maintenance. Non-confrontational resolution... You name it, I'm bad at it."

"Fine, then we'll focus on your strengths and start building on your weaknesses. You passed the trials, so you've got it in you. Now it's my job to nurture it and coax it out of you."

"Your aunt would argue. She took every chance she could to point out my failures in front of the other warriors. Honestly, I guess it's good that there are no other warriors because there's nothing you can say in front of Tundra that he hasn't already said to me himself."

I stand up and intercept his pacing. "I'll speak to him. If the four of us are building an army, I won't have anyone feeling belittled, no matter how intentional or unintentional."

I reach forward and offer him my hand. He stares at it at first, but after a long moment of hesitation, he meets me palm to palm.

"In the Human Realm, there is something called a do-over or a mulligan. It means you get to gather yourself and start fresh from where you are regardless of how badly you screwed up to get there. I'm giving you a mulligan, Dune. You're starting fresh from here, so work hard, try hard, and become the warrior you envisioned all those years as a kid in the desert."

Dune studies me as if searching for a sign this is a ploy or I'm about to burst out laughing and take it back.

I hold his gaze and offer him a smile. "You being a prick stops now. I mean it. I want this to work. In a way, we're all dating and getting to know one another. The four of us are bound. Accept that. Get over whatever insecurities or prejudices or competitive impulses you're having and show us a side of you we can get behind."

I wait until he nods and then touch the swelling on the split of his lip. "I'm sorry about this, but if you roll your eyes at me like that anymore, I'm likely to punch you again. I'm the fucking Princess of Dornte and the Guardian of the Crown. I deserve more respect."

He swallows. "You do, Princess. I'll do better."

"I know you will." Turning back, I pick up my chair and carry it to the wall where I found it. After setting it into place, I hold my hand out to him. "No man left behind, soldier. Remember that. This is a chance for a new beginning for all of us. Just try. I'll meet you halfway."

CHAPTER SIX

Lukas

*H*awk and I spend an hour interrogating Hunter and the goblin captured during Honor's attack. We end up with nothing new—a few insignificant pieces of intel, but not much more.

Hunter admits they fashioned the second portal gate and he imported the arsenal of illegal weapons he and Hawk's father stockpiled for years in the Human Realm.

He doesn't tell us where it is, though, so we're not much further ahead.

The goblin, Arlim Drace, admits his superiors targeted Honor to further weaken the Thornebane hold on the crown of Dornte.

He doesn't tell us anything of the plans yet to come and nothing that shakes loose can be used as actionable intel going forward.

"I say we lobotomize the fuckers." Hawk flashes me a mani-acal grin as he sinks onto the bench in the cell-keeper's office.

"We can donate their brain matter to science. Maybe they'll finally prove useful."

I plunk down on the seat next to him and tilt my head back against the wall. "Just not useful to us."

Hawk lights up one of his custom cigarettes and takes a long pull before offering me one too. I accept without hesitation and the two of us fall into a familiar pattern of decompressing.

His hand-rolled delights are strong enough to take the edge off a stressful day but not so strong that judgment is altered. Well, as long as we stop at one.

"What about dangling the possibility of conjugal sentencing in front of him?" I say. "He knows we have his bride behind locked doors, and he's headed into the same situation. Ravaging Raven might incentivize him."

Hawk exhales a long breath. "Honestly, I think him having a fuck buddy in prison is a good idea. I kinda like the idea of it being a guy named Rough Tom or Snake Bite and not his wife."

I laugh, but he's dead serious. "Fuck, this stuff smells good."

Hawk turns the heater of the cigarette toward himself as if considering that. "It took me a long time to perfect the blend."

I suck in another long pull and feel the stress of worrying about Honor subside a little—just a little.

"I know that look. That's woman worries." Hawk closes his eyes as if savoring this quiet moment. "How are things with the princess?"

"With her? Good."

"I sense a J.Lo-sized but coming."

I chuff. "Since when do we dish about women?"

"Since women took a front-row seat in our lives."

"Are you saying we're whipped?"

Hawk barks a laugh. "Oh, we're whipped, my friend. Make no mistake about that."

We both chuckle and then silence resumes.

I think about the stresses of the moment and the one thing

that's tying me up in knots. "I'm worried about the plot to eliminate her as a protector of the crown. She's barely out of her coma and goblins tried to kill her. I realize she's smart and capable of taking care of herself, but I'll feel a lot better when she's back to full strength."

"I remember that feeling too well. When Calli first came to us, she was so horribly unprepared for the dangers moving in on us. I nearly lost my mind."

I take another long draw and chuckle. "You *did* lose your mind—more than once. I remember prying your gun from your hand on more than one occasion."

Hawk chuckles. "It'll happen to you too. Love does that. Tosses you in a blender, dices you up, and liquefies even the toughest son of a bitch."

"Nah. I can't see that happening to me."

His grin widens. "You owe me a beer when it does."

Now it's me chuckling. "Hope you aren't thirsty because you'll be waiting for that beer."

He sits up and pinches his cigarette. "You saved me from myself more than once. Just know I'm here if you ever need a rescue and I can return the favor."

I finish my smoke break too and get back to it. "Don't be surprised if I take you up on that."

Tundra

I leave Honor to speak with Dune and hope she knows what she's up against. That man is infuriating beyond every sense of the word. I understand why she asked me to leave and it wasn't to be her messenger to Lukas. When I'm around Dune he's defensive and standoffish.

It's not the way I want things to be, but as roommates—first, when Valorous placed me with him to see if I could mold him into a soldier, and then at Mount Hekko when we were cast out for behavior unbecoming—we've fallen into a toxic rut.

I'm wandering through the maze of sub-level corridors when I realize I'm not sure where the prisoner holding area is. That makes connecting with Lukas more difficult. Unless...

I raise my wrist and tap through a few of the option buttons.

The widescreen changes and a dot appears with a compass arrow right below it. Perfect. I haven't learned everything there is about these tactical watches, but the Phoenix Quint, the royal four, and the four of us are all accessible by GPS tracking.

I pinpoint Lukas and strike off to see if I'm able to follow the breadcrumbs and track him down.

I exhale and try to release the tension that Dune inspires in me. The years of self-reflection taught me several things, but the point I struggle with most is how I failed Dune. There's a great soldier within him and I was tasked to bringing him to the fore.

I haven't.

I've tried genuine support, encouragement, tough love, being a hard ass, reverse psychology, honesty... but nothing gets through to him. His protective walls are so high and so strong, all I've managed to do is bash my head against the stone.

And what have I got to show for it?

A headache.

That's actually how our sexual relationship started too. I let him believe it's only ever been hate sex ignited out of frustration—and for the most part that's true—but that's not how it started.

When we first got together, I was making a genuine attempt on reaching him—not as his superior but as a male who cared about him.

That didn't go well. It became a game of push and pull and

now, even that has devolved into another way for us to attack one another.

When I arrive at the location where I'm pinging Lukas, I find him and Hawk chatting with the cell keeper.

"Hey, T," Lukas says, greeting me with an open palm. "How's things with our princess?"

"All is well," I say, nodding to Hawk and the castle security officer. "She wanted a moment to speak with Dune in private and asked that I let you know she is headed to Amberloq Hall for a few hours and that you should meet us there when it suits you."

"You could've texted me that."

I nod. "But she asked, so here I am."

Hawk chuckles. "Looks like you're not the only one whipped, my friend."

Lukas chuckles and points to the interrogation rooms. "Why don't you two have a go. Maybe changing up the interrogation team will shake something loose."

Hawk shrugs. "I'm game if you are, Dantos."

The male in uniform taps the screen of his monitor and steps around the console to join him. "Lead the way, Mr. Barron. Let us see what we can find out."

The click of the cell door closing brings a smile to Lukas's face. "And just like that, you and I are alone in a very private room."

I catch the look in his eye and the husky tone in his voice and look around. "What? Here? Now?"

Lukas chuckles. "Don't look so alarmed, Iceman. I'm not suggesting we get naked or lewd. I'm thinking we should capitalize on our shared moment this morning and keep that ember smoldering."

He's flirting with me again.

It's been so long since I interacted with a lover who is kind and nurturing, I almost miss the cues. "What do you have in mind?"

"Here, let me show you." Lukas raises his hand and curls his index finger toward himself. I follow the beckoning and meet him chest-to-chest. "Our kiss this morning has stayed with me. I'd like another."

So would I.

Our lips meet with a tenderness I'm unaccustomed to, a warmth I've been lacking for the past two years. Kissing Lukas isn't a battle for supremacy like it is with Dune. This is a show of affection... a shared attraction... a promise of what is to come.

His callused palm is rough against my jaw but gentle in touch. As his lips move over mine, his other hand wraps around my ribs and presses flat on my spine. The pressure on my vest is strong, yet not overpowering.

He'd let me back away if I want to.

I don't.

I wrap my arms around him as well, one hand dropping to his fine, muscled ass and the other crossing his back and crushing us chest to chest.

I have a few inches on him, but Lukas is tall for a human and our bodies fit together well... at least, so far.

Suddenly, I'm wondering if any of these prison cells are vacant and if we could use one to get naked and lewd. The possibility of that sends a rush of intent straight to my cock and I harden even more than I was.

There's no way he doesn't feel my arousal.

I certainly feel his.

Lukas groans, slowing the kiss and easing back with a smile. "That was perfection."

"Agreed. Are you sure it ends with just a kiss?"

He brings our mouths together again with a teasing smile

and catches my bottom lip between his teeth. He bites hard enough to sting but doesn't draw blood.

"Just a kiss for now. We're both on duty and we have like a hundred and fifty rooms at the Hall to christen later."

He searches my gaze and must read my confusion. "You don't know what that means?"

"I'm guessing it has something to do with us getting naked and sweaty."

"Very true. Humans have a playful tradition that when they move into a new house with a lover, they have sex in all of the rooms to christen their new home."

My cock twitches behind the buttons of my fatigues. "There are a lot of rooms."

He nods. "We better start as soon as possible. Otherwise, we'll never make it before the new Amberloq move in."

"And having sex in someone else's quarters might prove problematic."

He chuckles. "Maybe a little."

Before I ease back, I run my hand down the front of his pants. His cock is as solid as mine and I want to cast duty to the side and take advantage of it.

But we won't.

This is good too. The burn of anticipation will make things that much hotter later. "Thank you for the kiss."

He grins. "It was a damned good kiss."

"Looking forward to the next."

Lukas waggles his eyebrows. "Me too. Buuut until then, can I ask a favor?"

"Of course, what can I do for you?"

He steps back and pulls a computer drive out of his pocket. "Rhylan asked for some information one of our teams collected on possible rebel portal gate sites. Our USB tech doesn't interface with Dornte tech but we built an adaptor into a computer in the security office. Could you deliver this to him before you join Honor?"

I take the drive and lean in for one last kiss. "It'll cost you."

~

Shadow

"How's my favorite patient this morning?" Doc says, coming into my room. I follow the sound of his shoes on the floor but other than that cue, I have no way of knowing where he is in the world around me. "Are you feeling up to getting out of here?"

I follow the deep timbre of his voice as he moves up the side of my bed. "And where would I go?"

"Keyla and I are helping with the Amberloq Hall reopening and thought you might like to join us."

"As much as I support Honor in her destiny, what help could I offer?"

"Good company, sound judgment in a conversation, and, let's face it, you're easy on the eyes. We figured you might enjoy a walk through the forest. There's a breeze today and the blooms on the trees smell nice. Keyla says you enjoy the outdoors."

I close my eyes. "I don't suppose I'll be much of a woodland hiker anymore."

"Nonsense," Keyla says, joining us. "Nature is part of you at a cellular level. Elves have heightened senses, so once your body compensates for your visual deficit, I bet you won't be half as out of place as you're imagining in your frustrations."

"I'll take that bet and raise the stakes. Perhaps I can finance my life moving forward by banking on your optimism and winning the royal jewels."

She chuckles. "Don't be silly. Come, I brought some fresh

clothes from your suite. I promise you'll feel much better once you shower and change."

My first instinct is to balk and set my irritable side loose on her, but she is the queen and I am not a fan of wallowing.

One of the reasons I find myself so well suited to being a counselor is because an elf's logic center is stronger than emotional impulse. It is a boon in most situations although it does make it more difficult to date and cultivate deep connections.

People often misinterpret my reserved and dispassionate nature as me not being emotionally invested. I am. I simply express it differently than non-elven people.

Keyla helps me out of bed and down the hall to a small bathroom. She guides me forward and places my hands on the cool marble of the vanity counter.

"The sink is directly in front of you, the toilet four feet to your left, and the shower about the same distance to your right. Your clothes are here," she moves my hand to touch the pile, "and fresh towels here." She uses my other hand to place on top of a mountain of plush terry. "I'll turn on the water, set the temperature, and then let myself out. Any questions?"

I shake my head. "Not really. I suppose there has to be a first time for this. Ready or not, right?"

"Exactly. Unless you plan to never bathe again."

I chuckle. "I doubt that works into my long-range life goals."

"Good. Then we're making progress already. Take your time and if you need anything, just call out. Doc and I are in the office across the hall."

I stand with my hands on the vanity and nod at where the mirror would be in front of me. "I am certain I shall manage. Gratitude."

CHAPTER SEVEN

Tundra

The trip back to the security office passes in a blur of sexual emotion. The two times things have heated up with Lukas around were both about Honor—which was perfect at that time. But that kiss...

I stifle a groan and try to change my one-track mind onto another line of thought. It doesn't look good if a Biome General is marching through the castle with an obvious hard-on pressing on the front of his pants.

Thankfully, my fatigues are black and most people are too distracted by my wings to notice what's going on in my pants.

I stop at the new security door at the bottom of the basement step and enter my access code before pressing my palm against the scanner.

But that kiss...

Lukas knows how to lay one on a guy, that's for sure. When I'm through the door, I let myself revisit the feel of his lips on mine. I lift my fingers to my mouth and brush across the sensitive flesh.

My lips are still tingling with awareness.

I chuckle as my touch passes over the spot where he bit me. I look forward to repaying that little tease.

I'm halfway up the basement hall before it registers that Rhylan just ducked into the gym. I chuckle as I get to the door. "Do Dragons need to work out? I thought you were strong by nature."

"Never hurts to pump some iron," he says, leaning over to pick up the free weights.

Distracted as I am, it takes a moment for my mind to clear and realize something is off. "Hey, I was just with Lukas in the prisoner cells. He asked me to give you this. He said you were waiting for it?"

"Yeah. Great. Thanks."

I hand him the drive and leave him to his workout.

Anxious to join Honor at Amberloq Hall, I head back the way I came and... stall out at the access door at the bottom of the stairs. My instincts are firing off in every direction. Something feels off.

I'm still staring at the door to the castle proper when it beeps access granted for someone on the other side and opens. "Slecking hell, my man. You scared me. Why are you lurking in the hall?"

Rhylan saunters through the door and chuckles, patting his chest.

I hold up my finger. "Wait. Where did you just come from?"

"Uh... a private moment with Creed if you must know. Why?"

"Because I just had a conversation with you in the weight room. At least... I thought it was you."

The expression on his face darkens and he turns and bolts into a run.

Without understanding what's going on, I take chase and follow. The gym is empty and we continue to the security room. The two of us arrive at the door, but it's closed and locked.

Rhylan sets his hand over the security screen. "Access denied."

"Like hell, I'm denied." He pulls his tablet from his thigh pocket and starts tapping keys. "Tundra, while I override, you call backup. We've been breached."

"By whom?"

"My asshole twin."

Pulling out my tablet, I select Lukas's contact and hit video call. He's the closest one of us for backup and being with Hawk, one call will loop in the quint as well.

"Hey, T. What's up, mate?"

"Rhylan's twin has breached the security office and locked us out. He needs backup."

"Fuck! We're on our way and we'll call the quint."

I hang up and put away my tablet. This isn't the quint's fight but the Amberloq aren't ready to take on these kinds of conflicts alone. "Help is on the way."

Rhylan finishes what he's doing and hands me his tablet. Grabbing the door handle, he cranks it hard and shoulders the solid panel. When it gives way, he races straight for his mirror image sitting in one of the leather chairs in the corner sitting area.

Without stopping, he launches, flying through the air and grappling his brother around the chest. The thud of solid mass against solid mass precedes the chair toppling backward and two very angry siblings punching and scrambling and kicking on the floor.

The fight continues in a flurry of fists until heavy footsteps beat a hard rhythm up the corridor. A moment later, Lukas, Hawk, and then Brant join us.

"Should we break it up?" the bear asks, gun raised.

Lukas shakes his head. "Nah. We've got him covered. Let

Rhy get it out of his system. He deserves a few swings."

He does.

From what I've heard, Rhylan's brother and his mother attended his execution celebration and watched as he was tortured and set to be put to death for loving King Creed.

"Slecking asshole," Rhylan grunts, his chest heaving with exertion. "What were you doing in here, Vik? You know I'll figure it out, so tell me now and save us both the trouble."

"Can't a brother come to talk to his twin? Is there a law against that?"

"Yes. When you impersonate me and break into a secured section of the castle there are laws against that."

"Please. You and I practically built this security system. I hardly needed to break in. Although the new security door at the stairs was a bit of a challenge. Do you see the lengths I had to go, just to talk to you?"

"Nice try, asshole. Talking isn't one of your strengths. Lying. Betraying. Back-stabbing... those I would believe."

The two of them go back to cracking heads and bloodying knuckles and I look to the others. "And you're sure we shouldn't intervene?"

Lukas shakes his head, his gun still aimed. "No. We're here if anything goes south. I'm next in line, by the way. I owe him for the bullet he put in me."

"This the man who shot you at the sex club?"

Lukas nods.

Hawk frowns. "We prefer adult lifestyle club over sex club."

"My apologies." I'm confused. Why are we hashing out the semantics of hedonistic terminology instead of focusing on the security breach?

I'm about to ask that when Lukas smiles and pulls the trigger. A shot rings off and Rhylan's twin is thrown back over the overturned chair.

Hawk barks a laugh. "Feel better?"

"Yes, thank you." Lukas grins as he holsters his gun. "Revenge may not be the answer, but it is cathartic. I highly recommend it."

"And yet, you wouldn't let me shoot my brother this morning. How is that fair?"

"You wanted to kill him. I only want to inflict pain on Vikarus."

"A fine distinction."

"But an important one."

While the two of them chuckle about killing people, Rhylan sets the chair back on its legs and flops down into it to catch his breath. "Nice shot, by the way. Thanks for not hitting me."

Lukas grins. "One of the perks of working with a professional. You're welcome."

"You are all insane," Vikarus snaps. "I came in here to calm the waters and you've beaten me and shot me and accused me of hijacking your systems. I'm surprised you didn't call in an audience to watch me get abused."

"No," Rhylan snaps. "Only sadistic assholes pull up a chair to watch a man get tortured."

"We had no choice," Vikarus snaps. "I told you. Mom and I did what we could to help but all eyes were on us. You don't know how difficult the situation was."

"This is a very sad story," Brant says, pouting and pushing out his bottom lip. "I think I feel tears, coming on. Oh, nope. Just kidding."

"Why are you people here?" Vikarus scowls at Lukas, Hawk, and Brant. "Isn't castle security out of your wheelhouse? Shouldn't it be the Amberloq here to handle me? Where's Honor? I was hoping to run into her. You know, for old time's sake."

Hawk restrains Lukas and twists the warrior's gun out of his hand laughing about him owing him a beer.

As they spiral off in conversation, Rhylan searches Vikarus's pocket and retrieves the data drive I mistakenly gave him. "Not yours, jerk. And neither is this haircut. Why did you change it to look like me?"

"I miss us being the same. I figured it was faster for me to cut mine than to wait until yours grew back."

Vikarus's words are still resonating within me. *Shouldn't it be the Amberloq here to handle me?* There's something about the way he said that… "You wanted the Amberloq to respond."

The conversation dies down as all eyes turn on me.

I continue with my thought. "You sounded disappointed it wasn't the Amberloq who interceded. Why?"

"I'm not," Vik snaps. "I don't care about the Amberloq. I told you, I'm here to iron things out with my brother."

Hawk frowns. "Do you guys smell that, boys? That's the stench of, this dragon's full of shit and lying through his teeth."

Rhylan rises from his chair, steps into the washroom, and comes back carrying a towel. "You're bleeding on the floor. Don't."

Vik snatches the towel out of the air and scowls. "My mistake. I'll just tell this hole in my shoulder to suck it up."

"You do that."

I ignore the foolish banter. There's more going on here. I feel it. "Is this a test? Are you gauging response times? Numbers? Procedures? What do you want with the Amberloq forces?"

The veil of civility falls and Vikarus grins. "I think the better question is, what Amberloq force? Rumor has it, there is no force, and other than one peaker and one sandman seen fighting at the memorial ambush, the Amberloq seem to be wiped out."

Lukas grins. "Then our propaganda is working. The enemy are being lulled into a false sense of superiority. Excellent."

I don't like any of this. If he's here testing our numbers, there could be others invading Amberloq Hall.

Lukas seems to come to that conclusion at the same time as

me. His gaze hardens and he smacks Brant's shoulder. "Hawk and Rhy, you two have him. Brant and Tundra, you're with me."

The three of us leave the security office calmly, but the moment we're down the hall and through the doors to the castle proper, we burst into a dead run.

Dune

I'm not a jerk, am I? Okay, there's a part of me that knows the answer to that, and I don't like it. I definitely *can* be a jerk, but that's not who I am.

Not really.

I'm not one to go along with that psychobabble bull about delving into introspection. I am who I am, and contrary to what Honor thinks, I like who that is.

At least, for the most part.

As the two of us stride through the forest path, I prod my split lip and fight not to chuckle. The woman has a temper. That's good. I like a female with fire.

My lip is swollen and throbbing as if it has its own heartbeat.

That I could live without, but the heart-to-heart, however uncomfortable, was the first real moment the two of us shared. Sure, it started with the age-old impulse to punch my face, but it got better from there.

I think.

Honestly, it's hard to tell.

If I read the conversation right, she told me to straighten up and do better because she has faith I *can* do better. If I read it wrong, she might've told me to get my act together before I embarrass her and the Amberloq.

Either way, the takeaway is do better and become what the Amberloq and Princess Honor need.

I hope I can do that.

"Princess Honor," someone calls from behind us.

Honor stops to wait for the woman to approach. She has pink hair and is wearing loose-fitting clothes that give me no idea of what kind of physical threat she could pose. Or maybe that's just me being paranoid.

She's likely just someone she knows from the castle.

That theory ends the moment I get a look at Honor's face. This is a stranger to her.

The female seems innocent enough. She approaches with the proper amount of self-deprecating modesty and dips her gaze. "Princess. I noticed the activity at Amberloq Hall and wanted to offer my services. We've all heard rumors about how the Blood Witch destroyed the Amberloq force but if that's not true, it would be an honor to serve our guardians."

"In fact, it's not true. My general and I are on our way to continue readying Amberloq Hall right now. I will transition my army here permanently once the building is restored to its former glory. Our brave warriors have been away from the castle too long."

"Much too long," the girl says, turning her gaze on me. "You're one of them, aren't you?"

"I am Dune, General of the Desert Planes and—"

A glint of reflected light in the trees triggers my defensive instincts.

I flare my wings and spin, caging Honor against my body as the *pew-pew* of blaster fire rains upon us.

"What's happening?" Honor asks, her breath hot against my throat.

"We're under attack."

"Are you hurt?"

"My natural shielding helps. Weapon fire is uncomfortable but not painful. I need to evacuate you, though. When I straighten, I will scoop you into my arms and fly straight up through the canopy."

"No. I want to stay and fight."

"You're not armed and you aren't at full strength. For now, the tactical thing to do is get you to safety."

Before she has time to argue, I shift my hold on her and launch straight up and into the air. With my wings spread for flight, the enemy manage to land a shot to my calf but with my adrenaline pumping, it's no worse than a sandstorm burn.

"I'm taking you to Amberloq Hall to secure you, then I'll return to take care of the attackers."

"That girl we were talking to… was she a distraction to stop us in the crosshairs?"

"Likely, yes."

The wind whistles as I cut our path toward the massive mansion meant to house hundreds of Amberloq. The rooms are empty, but that needs to change.

"Just drop me," Honor says. "I'll secure myself. You go back and find that sniper."

"I can't just drop you."

"Of course, you can. There is an aerial entrance at the top of the rotunda. I may not have my full power yet, but I can spread my wings and land myself in my own house. Just line me up over the rotunda and drop me."

"As you wish, Princess."

When we get closer, she points toward the oculus at the peak of the center dome. "Do you see that glass, dome window?"

"Yes."

"It has a motion sensor that will pull back the glass and allow me entry into the dome room below."

"What if there are intruders within the hall?" I ask.

"The security protocols of the oculus room are locked against intruders. If there are already intruders in the house, I can seal the oculus and the dome room will become a panic room."

"How do you know this?" I ask.

She giggles. "When my aunt moved out, Amberloq Hall became my playhouse. I know every inch of that building."

Right. Of course.

As I drop lower, Honor kisses my cheek. "Be safe, Dune. Come back to me whole and healthy."

"I'll do my best, Princess. Be cautious."

Honor

Dune releases me and I fall from the protective warmth of his embrace. In the air, I pivot to face the circular glass window I pointed out to him and release my wings.

Wow, it's been years since I've been airborne.

Now that I am, I wonder how I survived so long without feeling the surge of energy I've always gotten from flying. Stretching out my arms, I dive, adrenaline pumping in my veins. It's like my body is coming alive again after a long hibernation.

I flap my wings and corkscrew in the air toward the oculus. My hair pulls in the wind and I laugh, throwing my head back, loving the rush of descent.

It strikes me a little too late that I should've slowed my descent to ensure the window would open. It's been a lot of years since anyone used this entrance.

My heart thunders against the cage of my ribs and I flare my wings to create some drag.

Shit. Shit. Shit. I'm going to hit hard. I'm going—

The glass turns clockwise and splits into pie wedge sections as it retracts. It's as exciting now as it was when I was ten and Creed and I used to play Hide-and-Seek in the mansion.

As cool as the oculus eye is, I'm more interested in what I will find inside. Once I'm through the domed opening, I scan the rotunda below and shift to land on my feet. The glass eye spins closed above and I cushion my landing by bending my knees.

With my feet on solid ground, I turn in the small space and face the security panel. It's not hard to find. The aerie room has a ten-foot diameter, with rounded walls, and a twenty-foot ceiling.

Effectively, it's like standing in the center of a silo.

I stop in front of the security panel and listen for any sign that the house has uninvited guests.

Despite what Dune, Tundra, and Lukas fear, I'm not as weak and helpless as they think. Sure, my muscles need strengthening and I tire easier than I used to, but I'm stronger every day.

I told Dune I *could* use this space as a panic room, but I won't. I'm not a shrinking violet and I certainly don't want to be up here hiding if there's not even anything to be worried about.

I tap the screen on the wall and see what I'm dealing with. It's one of the old security systems we used to have in the royal suite before Creed and I moved into the heirs' suite.

After bringing the system online, I punch in the failsafe code from when I was a kid. My father programmed a code for our family and I'm assuming, since we were the only ones who ever knew it, no one ever deleted it.

MONKEYNUTS

The system boots up and offers me an access list. Trailing a finger down the list of options, I access the room cameras and activate them.

The little screen breaks into quarters and I start toggling through the empty rooms. Four by four and then four more, I scan the interior of the mansion.

Tap. The fourth-floor corridors are empty.

Tap. Bedrooms empty. More empty bedrooms. More empty bedrooms.

Taptaptaptap. I continue with that on rapid-fire for way too long before I find something new to look at.

Tap. The main floor entrance is empty.

Tap. Kitchen, dining room, common room, and lounge empty.

I don't see anyone—*Tap.*

My stomach lurches as the camera comes on in the Guardian's library. *Shit.* Three goblins and a hipster white guy are tearing apart my library.

"They want the Amberloq discs," I say to myself. "Of course, they do. If they know I'm untrained and unprepared, it makes sense they want to take my only shot at becoming a decent Guardian of the Crown."

I rush forward and grab the door but then think better of it.

"I'm the biometric key to unlocking the sealed chamber. If they don't have me, they're screwed. If I run down there and get myself captured by four guys, then they'll be able to force the locks open."

Look at me cooking with gas.

With that in mind, I go back to the security panel. "Okay, so..." I push the button to seal the oculus against entry and lock the doors, sealing myself in and away from my intruders. "Take that, assholes."

I scroll back to the screen of the library at the same time the tactical watch Lukas makes me wear starts vibrating like mad. I turn my wrist to read the incoming message, but I don't understand how the thing works or what I'm supposed to do.

"Damn. I need a lesson on how to work my watch."

Shadow

Doc and Keyla are kind enough to tend to me while I get my bearings in the forest and honestly, Keyla is right. Even with everything changed about the way I perceive the world visually, being in nature feels as welcoming and natural as it ever has.

"How are you feeling?" Keyla asks.

"Isn't that usually my line?"

She chuckles and squeezes my arm where we're linked at the elbow. "Your sense of humor is returning. That's a good sign."

"In truth, I am much more content out here than I was lying in bed thinking about what I've lost."

"So, maybe think about what you've gained?" Dillan says.

I turn to my right and stare blankly at the place I hear him walking beside me. "And what shall I consider my first boon? Stubbed toes? Elves don't usually trip over roots or need an escort through forested paths."

"No, but now you can experience nature on another plane. I've seen the hydroxyecdysone levels building in your cells. Something incredible is happening to you."

"I doubt incredible is the correct descriptor, but I appreciate your point."

"Shadow?" Keyla squeezes my arm and pulls us to a stop. "The way you said that sounds like you know what's happening. Do you?"

I draw a deep breath. There's no reason not to confide in them. They are close friends and neither would betray my trust. Besides, if I'm right, they shall know soon enough.

"I do. Or, at least, I think I do."

"All right," Doc says. "Care to fill your doctor in?"

"Apologies, Doc. As much as it has been a shock to me, I should have confessed my truths to you as soon as I realized what might be happening."

"Apology accepted. So, what is happening?"

I swallow and summon the courage to speak the words I have never spoken in all my life. "I am only half urban elf.

Though I display the characteristics of my father's side, I am fairly certain the mutations in my cells come from my mother's DNA activating within me."

"Wait," Doc says. "I never said mutation. Your cells are metamorphizing but that—"

"I consider it a mutation. It certainly will change how people see me and interact with me."

"Why?" Keyla asks. "What is it? What DNA did your mother carry that you find so offensive?"

I close my eyes and let the words fall from my tongue. "My mother, though I have never met her, is an Ordained Oracle."

The two of them go agonizingly quiet.

"Wow," Doc says. "That's... wow."

"Shadow..." Keyla says, her voice as soft as a feather's brush, "you being born of a union with one of the ancients of the oracle world is incredible. It's rare... unheard of, actually."

"Rare, yes, but it does happen. The rarer thing is that my maternal side is surfacing this late in life. As a half-breed, the oracle traits should have been dominant over my elven traits, if I were born with any."

"Well, obviously, you're a late bloomer," Doc says, "because, yeah, this makes so much sense."

"I was denounced by the oracles at birth. My father never told another soul what my mother was. If the premonitions and clairvoyance surface, I will be ostracized from my elven family as well. Without proper training, the invasions of my mind will very likely drive me insane. So, for me, this is nothing to celebrate."

"Oh, Shadow." Keyla squeezes my arm. "We won't let that happen. If your oracle powers are surfacing, surely your mother or her people will want to train you."

"No. You see, I lived my entire life among the chaos of the common folk. In the eyes of both my ancestral species, I am now tainted and unwanted."

"Well, fuck them," Doc says. "I don't know a thing about being an Ordained Oracle or how to help you, but I'll die trying. I'll call in every favor I've got owing and we'll figure something out. Hell, with Hawk and Kotah and Creed on board, we've got this."

"I appreciate your support, Doc, but you have yet to see how this will affect me. It is more of an affliction than a gift. Odds are you and Keyla and everyone else will want to get as far away from me as possible."

"Not going to happen," Keyla says, hugging my arm tight. "I'm telling you right now, Shadow. You are not alone in this. Don't give up on us because there's no way we're giving up on you."

"Hell no," Doc says, a strong hand squeezing my shoulder, "but you gotta be straight with us and tell us how to help you. We admit we know nothing about what's happening to you, but we are in it to win it. Wait and see. We'll manage this together."

Oh, I will see all right.

I will see everything I never wanted to know about everyone around me.

The three of us strike off again toward Amberloq Hall. We've barely gotten a hundred feet before someone steps in our path and Doc's bear begins to growl.

"Majesty, how lovely of you to join our fun. Follow our instructions and no one else needs to die."

CHAPTER EIGHT

Tundra

The moment Lukas, Brant, and I are clear of the castle, I take flight and pump my wings as if Honor's life depends upon it. Maybe it doesn't but the twisting deep in my gut tells me there's more to Rhylan's twin showing up than rebuilding burned bridges.

Why lock the door to the security office and raise the alarm if he didn't want to draw maximum attention?

He was testing our defenses.

I race across the treetops of the forest between the castle and Amberloq Hall, my emotions vacillating between my duty to protect the Guardian of the Crown and my need to protect Honor, the female who is making space for me in her life and her bed.

She is truly exquisite, inside and out.

And then there's Lukas...

My mind is about to career off on a sexual tangent when I catch sight of Dune diving into the canopy.

He's a pain in my ass more often than not, and reckless and

disrespectful more often than that, but the look on his face is focus and determination.

I follow his trajectory and burst through the leaves and branches just as the laser fire begins below.

Pivoting to avoid a bolt of energy, I take in the scene. Dune has engaged with two hostiles while more are battling with Doc's black bear and Keyla's wolf.

In the midst of it all, Shadow is kneeling on the ground blind and helpless.

As I descend, I go through my options. My first duty is to secure Keyla and protect the crown. In her wolf form, I'm not sure I can scoop her up and remove her from the battle.

Would her wolf know me? Do wildlings share their body with another entity or do they simply take another form? I don't know and I don't have time to ask.

Both she and Doc are deeply entwined in a melee fight, so I can't be sure to evacuate her without causing one or both of them injury.

I should join the fight and assure Queen Keyla's safety that way.

With that worked out, I tuck my wings back and gain speed on my approach. At the last moment, I flare my wingspan and use the backward pull to swing my legs forward and kick.

My boots connect and a goblin is hurled back into the trunk of a nearby tree. The crack of bone and lack of response tells me he is not getting up from that.

Ever.

Keyla has another man by the throat and shakes her head, whipping the man like a rag doll as she prowls backward on all fours. Blood is spraying from his wounds and staining her stunning, white coat, but she doesn't even seem to notice.

Dillan has reared onto his back legs and towers over the two he's defending against. His paws swipe through the air, long, chestnut claws tearing through flesh.

Bang. Bang. Bang.

Three goblins fall to the dirt.

I spin to find Lukas standing, gun extended, his stance braced. I snap the neck of the one I'm battling and the forest quiets.

Dune finishes with his opponents and gives us a nod. "Hey, how's your day going?"

"Where's Honor?" Lukas asks, racing in to join us.

"When the first wave of attack started, I evacuated Honor to Amberloq Hall. There is a secret entrance through the oculus of the rotunda and she intended to lock herself down. Then, I came back to deal with these snotgoblins."

Keyla and Doc reclaim their human forms and rush to check on Shadow.

"Was the mansion secure?" Lukas asks.

"I don't know. I didn't see anyone there, but I also didn't hang around to check. Either way, Honor is safe and secured."

"Provided she really did lock herself down instead of investigating the house and taking a stand."

"Yeah. Provided she listened and didn't engage."

The three of us look at each other and frown.

"Off you go, boys," Lukas says. "We'll be right behind you."

I assess the queen's safety and decide she's in no imminent danger.

"We're good," Doc says, obviously understanding my conflict. "Go check on Honor. Like Lukas says, we're right behind you."

Dune and I push off and within moments are setting down on the front walkway of Amberloq Hall.

"How do you want to do this?" Dune asks. "If there are trespassers, walking in the front door is likely to give us away pretty quickly."

I shrug and wrap my wing forward to curl around my front like a cape. "This is meant to be our home. If there are trespassers, they are the ones who don't belong, not us. I say, we go in and take them out."

"How very direct of you. I like it. Here. I grabbed these from the ones I took care of. Which one do you want, rifle or blaster?"

"I'll take the hand blaster."

Dune hands me the weapon and I check the settings, the bolts remaining, and the power charge. There is still plenty of everything. I finish with my assessment and nod. "Let's have some fun."

~

Lukas

When Tundra and Dune take off, I scan our surroundings and double-check the state of deadness of the raiding party. After texting Rhylan that we took out an ambush squad in the forest, I check in with Keyla and Doc. "Are you ready to move out?"

"Ready," Keyla says, linking her arm around Shadow's elbow. "Well, this has been an exciting first walk in the forest, hasn't it?"

The elf looks miserable. I don't blame him. Feeling vulnerable and powerless sucks ass. It couldn't have been fun to be at the mercy of the world around you knowing everyone else was fighting.

I make a mental note to work with him on spatial defense in the future. He might be blind but he is by no means helpless.

The four of us make quick work of cutting through the forest path to the mansion.

"Aside from the ambush," I say, "this was a much easier trek than the other times we've come."

Keyla nods. "The brownies mentioned they've been working hard to ready the Hall for you four to move in."

"I knew they were helping in the house, but I didn't realize they were landscaping too."

"They are an amazing workforce. The harder they can work, the happier they are."

Yeah, there aren't a lot of species like that.

When we get to the iron gate, I point to the bent and cut rungs and signal for Keyla to hang back with Shadow. After drawing my gun, Doc and I enter to check things out and get a lay of the land.

Everything seems quiet inside...

"Have they come and gone?" Doc asks me in a hushed whisper.

"Stick close to Keyla and Shadow. Give me a sec to move in and see what I can find out." Without waiting for his response, I squeeze through the broken gate and jog up to the side of the building.

The place is massive. Whoever forced their way in here could find a hundred hiding places inside.

The smash of glass behind me has me pivoting, gun raised. The goblin that crashes to the stone patio lands with a dull thud and doesn't move.

Dune leans out onto the sill of the window. "And stay out, you piece of shit."

"More coming your way," Tundra says from inside.

Dune ducks back inside and then two more intruders are thrown out. I assess the stillness of them lying there and figure they are either dead or have been stunned by a powerful weapon.

I round the front of the house and wave Doc in. "It seems Dune and Tundra are taking out the trash and given that they didn't seem overly rushed about it, I assume they've got things mostly under control."

"Was there any doubt?" Dune says, opening the front door.

"Although, according to Honor, a few bolted out the back when we got here."

I pull out my phone and connect with the security office. "I'll have Rhylan send out guards to search and secure the grounds for any stragglers."

Once I've sent that text, I climb the front steps and wave Keyla in with Shadow. "What are you doing with the three you threw out the window? Will they still be out by the time castle security teams get here?"

Dune grins. "They'll be out for hours."

I jog up the stairs and into the house. "And Honor told you a few bolted? So, you confirmed she's safe?"

"Perfectly," she says, sweeping into the entrance. "Dune delivered me from danger and told me to lock down and, I did as I was told without argument."

Despite her assurance, I study her as she approaches.

She knows what I'm doing and smiles at me as if a light is turned on, illuminating her from within.

"Why do you look so radiant?"

"Because I flew for a bit to enter the house from above and I connected to the security system without issue and I made a sound, strategic decision in the heat of the moment that shows true promise for me being an Amberloq leader."

I chuckle as she walks right up to my chest and wraps her arms around the back of my neck. I give her a quick kiss and lean back to meet her purple gaze. "You've been a busy girl. Let me hear your sound strategy. I want to bask in your glory."

She waggles her brow. "Well, my base instincts screamed for me to challenge the men trying to break into the library, but then I realized that by not giving them access to me and my biometrics, I was more effective in foiling them by staying put than by engaging."

"Solid and strategic," I say, fingering a strand of silver off her cheek and behind her ear. "Well done."

"Thank you. It was the first time I truly felt in control of a terrible situation instead of overwhelmed."

"That is wonderful," Shadow says, entering the house on Keyla's arm. "I wish I could say the same."

I remember what Honor said last night about Shadow feeling stronger when hearing about her trials and triumphs and decide now would be a great time to revisit that for his sake. "You mentioned the intruders trying to get into the library?"

"The Guardian's chamber of the library, yes."

I point toward the community room and then to Shadow. "Why don't you, Keyla, and Shadow head into the community room. They were attacked on the way here and could likely use a moment to decompress. I'm sure they'd also like to hear about your epiphany and what that means going forward."

Honor smiles, catching my drift. "That's a great idea. I already told Tundra what I saw on the monitors. He can catch you up on what the intruders were touching in the library."

"Perfect. We'll be in shortly."

Honor

It doesn't take a genius to understand what Lukas wants and why. Shadow is obviously shaken and if they were attacked in the forest, his sightlessness would've seemed even more terrifying and debilitating than it did while lying in bed.

"Despite Lukas's positive thinking, I don't think the bar has been fully stocked—Oh! My mistake." I round the square of four tufted, leather couches facing one another and head over to the long bar. "It seems the castle brownies have gone over and above. The bar is open. What can I get you?"

Doc comes in, scans the room, and strides forward to join

me. "I know how to make Keyla's drink of choice. Do you mind if I join you back there?"

"By all means, there's plenty of room for two."

Shadow sits back on the couch and rests his arm over the arm. "I would take a beer, ale, mead, or anything of the kind."

"I'm sure there is. Yes, you're in luck." I get Shadow set up and crack open a beer for myself while Doc takes care of himself and Keyla. Walking back over to the square of couches, I take a seat next to Shadow. "Here you go."

He opens his hand and I press the bottle into his palm. Without pause, he lifts the rim to his lips, swallows hard and fast, and upends it down his gullet.

When he finishes, he takes a moment to swallow and then nods. "Gratitude."

Eyes wide, I take in Keyla's surprised expression and shrug. "That kind of night, is it?"

Doc joins us, carrying his drink, Keyla's, and a second beer for Shadow. "Here you go, my friend. Looks like you're looking for a little liquid sedation tonight."

"You may be right," he says, holding up his empty hand and closing his fingers around the icy dew of the second bottle. "Gratitude."

"Not a problem. The best part of drinking it off with friends is that you don't need to explain or worry about what comes next. Whatever happens tonight, we've got you, so have at it."

I'm not sure what I've missed, but something tells me Doc and Keyla have the full story.

Whatever it is, Shadow is trying to drown it out.

Fine by me. I've been there a few times in my life.

"You do you, Shadow," I say. "I've got two hundred and fifty beds upstairs. You're welcome to claim any one of them."

"Do they have mattresses?" Doc asked. "We came to see if we could help with the restoration, but this place looks incredible."

I couldn't agree more. "From what I saw from the security

cameras when I was panning through rooms and searching for intruders, many of the rooms are ready to be occupied. We need all the final touches, but we've got the basics covered."

"That's wonderful," Keyla says. "I'll have the housekeeping staff set you up with linens and toiletries as soon as I get back to the castle."

"Thanks, I appreciate that." I smile at my brother's wife. She, Doc, and Shadow were attacked in the forest, and yet, Keyla is as well-put-together as any queen you could ever meet.

Nothing seems to rattle her cage.

"Has Creed been out flying lately?"

Keyla blinks and looks at Doc. The two of them shake their heads. "Not that I'm aware of. Laryssa had his wings shorn when she took him prisoner. They only grew back on the day of his coronation."

"What?" I raise a hand to my throat and fight to swallow my beer. "I didn't know that."

"Not many people do. That's why he wears them out so often. For two years he believed he wasn't a true fae and never would be again. Having his wings restored has done great things for his confidence in assuming the crown. He honestly didn't think the citizens would accept him without them."

How heartbreaking.

I realize, once again, how little I know about my brother's suffering during our two years of captivity. The guilt and shame of my judgment could swallow me if I let it. I was so caught up in my own suffering...

Keyla leans forward in her seat and reaches over to place her hand on mine. "Honor? Are you all right?"

A rush of serenity seeps across my skin and I meet her kind, chestnut gaze. "I am truly, so sorry. I've been such a bitch to you and Creed, and I didn't even take the time to meet you, Doc. I'm sorry. I feel awful."

Keyla swallows and waves that away. "No, don't. Please. This is where we are, right now, and it's good. I didn't mention Creed's suffering to make you feel bad. My point was that he only just recovered his wings and as far as I know, hasn't taken the opportunity to soar the sky yet."

"Well, I'd like to change that. He and I used to enjoy flying together. We should definitely take the opportunity very soon."

Keyla's smile is so genuinely warm, my guilt takes another run at me. "He will love the idea. You should."

Doc lifts his arm and frowns. "We're getting called back by Rhy. Creed heard about the attack and is in a bit of a panic. He can't leave the meeting with the quadrant leaders but asks that we come back and prove to him we're unharmed."

Keyla rolls her eyes and chuckles. "He's such a protective worrier, your brother."

"He is."

Doc takes his and Keyla's glasses and sets them in the sink at the bar. When he comes back, he offers Keyla a hand up. "Shadow? What's your plan, buddy? Do you want to come back with us to the castle or stay here for a bit and get a change of scenery?"

"You're welcome to stay and day drink," I say. "We planned to be here all day working and making ourselves at home. Since the work seems to be pretty much complete, we might as well enjoy the place."

"If it is not an imposition, I would very much like to stay and get drunk."

"Then drunk you shall get," I say, nodding to my brother's mates. "We're good."

Keyla looks concerned but doesn't argue.

Hey, let the man deal in his own way. When she steps toward the door to leave, she tilts her head and signals for me to join them. "Give me two seconds to walk them out, Shadow. Then we'll gather the guys and see who wants to join us."

"Take your time," Shadow says, raising his beer. "I am in good company."

I follow the two of them out to the front entrance and then further still to the other side of the door to stand on the porch.

Doc closes the door behind us and leans in close. "Shadow confided in us about what's happening to him. He might be ready to talk about it with you too. Try to get him to open up. But if he doesn't and anything concerning happens, call me, day or night."

"Concerning?" I repeat. "What does that mean?"

Keyla smiles and squeezes my arm. "Not our story to tell, but Doc's right. Day or night. If Shadow needs us, we're here for him."

"Okay. I'll keep that in mind. And thanks for looking out for him. He's a good guy."

"A great guy," Keyla says. "Take good care of him."

"We absolutely will."

CHAPTER NINE

Tundra

I catch a brief portion of Honor's whispered conversation as I finish securing the perimeter. I stop before intruding and wait until Doc and Keyla strike off toward the castle once more. "Is everything all right, Princess?"

Honor startles a little and then chuckles. "Fine. I was just wondering if we should be concerned about letting them go alone in the woods."

"No. They are safe enough. There is a squadron of castle guards combing the trees. The goblins we took down have been removed and the dead have been taken to the lab for forensics to go over. Maybe we can get a location of where they came from or who they are. Either way, the danger has passed for now."

Honor sighs and leans into my side. "For now."

She's tired and it does my heart good to have her lean on me for comfort and strength. "What were they saying about Shadow and concerning things happening? Is he ill? I thought his blindness was the only challenge since he regained consciousness."

"It is, as far as I know. He needs a little camaraderie and seems intent on getting good and drunk to wash away his troubles."

"I'd say he deserves a bender," Lukas says, coming around the house with tools in hand. "We all deserve it."

"Is the window repaired?" I ask, pleased that Honor has remained nuzzled against my side even with the appearance of Lukas.

He points his hammer back the way he came and shrugs. "Boarded up but not fixed. Still, I spelled it as well. It'll keep bad guys out for the night."

"Excellent." I gesture to the front door and shift my hold on Honor to lace our fingers and hold her hand. "Then we're all set to get our drunk on."

"What-what?" Dune says, jumping over the railing of the fourth-floor in the grand entrance. He flares his wings as he descends and lands in a graceful crouch.

When he straightens, he seems more relaxed than I've seen him in years. It looks good on him.

He flexes his shoulders and settles his feathers. "Did my ears deceive me or did I hear our stern and serious Iceman refer to letting loose?"

Honor chuckles. "You did. We were discussing locking the mansion down and day drinking like you read about."

"Excellent idea. The first round is on me."

Dune strides off toward the common room and I shake my head. "Dune being this excited is never a good sign. I am afraid."

Dune barks a laugh. "I heard that, Frosty. Come on. Thaw out a little."

"The Quint calls it a drink and think," Lukas says. "They get their libations flowing and brainstorm the problems swirling and threatening to suck everyone down the drain."

Honor jogs over to the bar, her silver hair shimmering against her backside. "My gods, she has a beautiful ass," I whisper to myself.

"No argument," Lukas says, watching her across the room. "We'll circle back around to that later. Right now, we've got company."

"I like the sound of circling back," I say, meeting his gaze. "And thank you for earlier. For the kiss and the promise of more, and also for supporting the growth of a bond between Honor and me. The moment the magic triggered, and I realized I was destined to be a Guardian General, I wondered how it would work. You've made things much easier than they could've been."

He turns to face me and my blood pumps a little harder. What is it about him that stirs things inside me?

"The way I see it, Honor is the primary person in this destiny, so it's not my place to try to upstage her or change that. She has a pivotal role to play and needs continuity and support."

I hold up my hand between us and he accepts the offer and clasps hands with me. "You are an impressive male, Lukas. I see why Honor fell in love with you."

His smile is soft as his gaze finds our girl delivering a round of drinks to the couches. "Love? Do you think we're there?"

"That's what it looks like from the outside. Is that not where you are?"

"Me? Oh, hell yeah. I was a goner before she even woke up from her coma. I just don't want to rush her."

Honor looks up from her conversation with Shadow and the moment her gaze locks with Lukas, her entire aura starts to glow.

"You're not rushing her. That girl radiates love."

~

Shadow

By the fourth ale, the jagged edges of my self-pity are being chipped away and I'm starting to relax. By the fifth, the world seems a little less horrifying. Honor is good company. The others are as well, just without the sexy voice... well, that's not true either.

Tundra's deep voice and Lukas's accent are both very stirring. How lucky they found one another.

"All right," Lukas says, chuckling about something. "In the spirit of a true Jaxx Stanton drink and think, I propose we each down a round of Haze shots and then start a party game. Does anyone have a preference?"

"Cards Against Humanity is hilarious," Honor says, "but Tundra and Dune wouldn't understand the Human Realm references and Shadow can't read them. Still, I vote for something like that."

Lukas barks a laugh. "So, something morally telling and off-color."

"Yup, that's how I roll when I'm drinking."

I laugh. "See, things are being revealed already."

Honor laughs. "Oh, speaking of things being revealed. You know that song, Tequila Makes Her Clothes Fall Off?"

Lukas groans. "Jaxx may have played it a hundred times over the course of our tour bus travels."

"That's how I roll when I drink, so beware."

Lukas barks a laugh. "Is that supposed to be a warning or an invitation to get you drunker?"

"That's not for me to judge. Just don't say I didn't warn you. Drunk Honor is a bit of a wild woman and she's not fond of clothes."

"Here's to Drunk Honor," Dune says. "I look forward to meeting her."

"I think we all do," Lukas says. "Here, let me pour another round of shots."

"Back to the drinking game," I say, shifting on the couch to face the place where Honor is seated. "What about a basic truth or dare? It would be a good way to get to know your new mates."

"I'm game," Honor says. "We'll start there. Generals, listen up. The gist of the game is when it's your turn, you get to pick whether to answer truthfully to one poignant question or act out a dare. You have only those two choices. Truth or dare."

Tundra laughs. "Thus the name."

"Exactly."

"All right," Tundra says, "That sounds simple enough. I'm in."

"Me too," Dune says. "I think I'll like this game."

"Blind man starts," I say, holding out my glass. Being drunk and feeling the room spin and not being able to see anything to anchor myself is a very unusual feeling.

I rather enjoy it.

"Are you milking our pity to get the lead on this?" Lukas asks.

"Absolutely. Also, the blind man needs a refill."

"Got you covered, elf," Lukas says. "What's your call, truth or dare?"

"Truth."

"All right," Honor says. "Let's start off easy. What is the most inappropriate time you ever got turned on and did you act on it?"

I think about that for a moment and chuckle. "I used to offer counseling at group sessions in the Prime Palace. One time, a siren was discussing how her need for sex was having a detrimental impact on her life in the human world. She went on to describe in great detail how she craved men filling her, and fondling her nipples, and coming in her mouth. I admit, I had to set my tablet in my lap and wait to adjourn for coffee or run the risk of embarrassing us both."

"After the meeting, did you act on it?" Dune asks.

"With her? No. That would've been highly unprofessional."

The couch dips beside me and Honor chuckles. "But you did act on it."

"Alone in my office once everyone left. Yes, I absolutely did."

"Yeah, you did. And that's how it's played, boys," Lukas says, touching my hand. "Here's your next drink, my friend."

"All right, Lukas next," Dune says.

"Truth or dare, Lukas?" I ask.

"I'm game. Your pick."

"All right," Honor says. "Truth. If you had to choose between going through life naked or having your thoughts appear in bubbles above your head for everyone to read, which would you choose?"

"Thought bubbles. People pretty much know what I'm thinking anyway. I'm not one to mince words."

"Too easy," Dune says. "I have a question."

"Shoot," Lukas says in response.

"You and Shadow spent weeks together in the heirs' suite working to help Honor. Was there ever a spark? You're both very pretty. In my mind's eye, I have the two of you naked and nailing to pass the time."

"Oh," Honor says beside me. "I never thought about it, but yeah, good question. Did the two of you ever get naked and nail?"

Lukas chuckles. "Shadow is obviously a very attractive man. He's smart, kind, and looks great with a towel wrapped around his hips. Was there ever a spark? No. Do I consider him worthy of a spark? Absolutely. The opportunity just never came up. We were focused on Honor and her well-being."

My cheeks warm as the room seems to heat up.

Lukas finds me attractive? That's news to me.

"All right, I call a dare for Lukas," Tundra says.

Lukas laughs. "Guys, this isn't how it's played. We're supposed to go around to everyone, not give me three turns in a row."

"Do Tundra's dare and you can skip two turns around the room," Honor says. "I'm curious to hear what he's got in mind."

"All right," Lukas says. "What's on your mind, T?"

"I'd like to give you the chance to spark. Having had the pleasure of kissing you, I can honestly say, you excel at it."

"Thank you. That's nice of you to say."

"You earned the compliment. Believe me. So, if Shadow doesn't object, I dare you to crawl into his lap and kiss him with all the passion and attraction you feel."

Honor's breath escapes her lips beside me as she gasps. "A great dare, Tundra. Uh-huh, I want to see this too. Shadow? Are you game?"

My heart picks up as my pulse races double time. "I chose the game for us to play, so it would be bad form to balk at the first dare. Yes, bring it on, Lukas. Unleash some of that mage magic on me."

"All right," Lukas says, amusement thick in his voice. "Tundra, hold my drink."

There's a shift of positions in the square of couches and then Lukas takes my drink from my hand. "Honor, if you will?"

"My pleasure." She shifts to take it beside me.

"Crawl into his lap, eh?" Lukas repeats.

"Yes." Tundra's voice has dropped an octave and the scent of sexual arousal is growing stronger in the air.

I scoot away from the arm of the couch and hold my hand up to meet his body as he approaches. "Dune's question was not aimed at me, but I noticed you as well. You are a ruggedly attractive male with a chiseled body honed by military service and the most beautiful hazel eyes I ever had the pleasure to fall into."

"Oh, now you're just flirting with me." Lukas slides a knee up my right hip and then another up my left.

At a loss for how I should respond to this, I let the alcohol lead my course and succumb. My throat is dry and I swallow. It does nothing to settle my racing nerves.

"And you smell nice," I add. "You always smell so good."

Lukas

Fuck me. What started out as a harmless frat house drinking game to cheer up a friend has morphed into a hot and heavy voyeuristic moment. And, if I'm being totally honest, I'm not thinking about Shadow as a friend right now.

What happened to him over the past days and weeks is terrible and I feel compassion for him. But the weeks before that, he and I grew close and I feel something altogether different for him too.

"Is stalling part of this game?" Dune asks.

Right. Less thinking, more kissing.

Cupping his smooth-skinned jaw in my palms, I tilt his mouth up to meet mine. "Shadow, take from me that which is freely given." The elven oath of affection rolls off my tongue with conviction as I lean forward, claim his lips, and press him into the back of the couch.

The spark they were hoping for ignites immediately. My body responds the moment our lips touch and I'm swept up in the drunken haze of kissing someone I care about who desperately needs to be kissed.

As his lips move over mine, I swipe the seam of his mouth and am gratified when he opens up.

Fuck, he tastes good.

Like haze and beer and hunger. It's a heady trifecta.

Sure, I'm buzzed and more than a little wound up after a wild day, but being like this with Shadow does something to me.

I shift my hold from his jaw to slide up the lengths of his ears and start stroking the gentle peaks. He shudders beneath me, his cock hardening against mine as I bend him backward.

Fuck, I'm practically crushing him into the cushion.

My mind is spinning.

Something in the back of my brain reminds me that this is only supposed to be a playful kiss—a challenge—but I want it to be more.

I wish it could be.

But this isn't that.

Life is complicated enough for Shadow as it is.

I slow the kiss and ease back, my heart racing like a caged beast beneath my collared shirt. Climbing free of his lap, I reclaim my drink and sit where I'd been before the challenge.

The room is silent.

Honor, Dune, and Tundra are studying me, wide-eyed and with far too much interest for my liking.

I sit back and raise my drink. "What? You said kiss him and let the spark ignite. I did. Why are you staring?"

Honor blinks and breaks into a smile. "First off, that was seriously one of the hottest kisses I've ever seen. I'm wet and I was just watching. Second, are you sure that was the first time you two connected because holy shit that was more than a spark."

I chuckle. "That was the first time."

Shadow raises his fingers and touches his lips. "But not your first time kissing an elf. You have definitely pleasured a member of my race before."

"What makes you so sure?" Honor asks.

Shadow swallows. "He began with the oath of affection and ended with fondling the peaks of my ears. Those are two very telling details that only someone with intimate knowledge of my culture would know."

Honor passes Shadow his beer and sits back on the couch they're on to study me. "Do tell, Mr. Mage. Who was she?"

I shake my head. "No comment. The deal was, I get to skip the next three rounds because I played the last three. I believe it's your turn, Princess. Truth or dare?"

"After seeing you devour Shadow, definitely dare. Come on boys, make it good."

I chuckle and think about that. "All right, in the interest of getting to know you better. I dare you to send each one of us a dirty text. It has to be either what you want to do to us or want us to do to you. And, for Shadow's sake, you can whisper in his ear."

She arches a brow with a challenging smile warming her face and then finishes her drink. "All right. Grab me a refill. This will take a minute."

CHAPTER TEN

Honor

I wake, lying on my side on a bare mattress with a foot in front of my face and a hand up my shirt. The fog and fuzz in my brain tell me this is the morning after the night before and I groan and let my eyes fall closed.

"Good morning, Princess," Dune says, his voice a deep whisper against my ear. He releases his hold on my boob and eases his morning wood away from the crack of my ass. "Sorry about the groping. Unintentional morning arousal, I assure you."

I hug my arm over his and put his hand back where it was. "I wasn't complaining."

It occurs to me that the best way to break through Dune's bravado and bullshit might be to start sharing real moments with him. Yesterday in the gym we seemed to come to an understanding.

This seems like the perfect time to add to it.

"So, you're saying that column of marble pressing against my ass has nothing to do with me?"

The deep-throated chuckle vibrates from his chest to my back. "I said unintentional, not unrelated."

"So, if it was meant for me, intentional or not, any chance you'd like to put it to good use?"

"Waste not, want not."

I smile, thankful for the playful ease of the morning. I lift my head to see who the foot belongs to. The white feathers tell me it's Tundra.

"Don't mind him," Dune whispers. "He's surprisingly ill-equipped to handle drinking for a big guy. He'll be out for a while yet."

It wouldn't matter to me if he wakes up, but honestly, it's nice to have a little one-on-one with Dune.

Shifting my shoulder, I make enough room to roll onto my back and look him in the eyes. The first thing I notice is that I went to sleep in my underwear and Lukas's t-shirt. I vaguely remember shedding my clothes as the drinking games progressed, but don't remember how I ended up wearing this.

Regardless, nearly naked works for me right now.

The second thing I notice is that I don't recognize the room we're in. "Where are we?"

"One of the bedrooms. We tried to steer you to the master suite, but you gave up in the corridor outside and crawled onto this bed."

I don't remember that.

"A bed is a bed, I guess. And more importantly, it puts us in a position to put this bad boy to use. Shall we?" I cup my palm against the front of his underwear. "I'll strip you. If you want to strip me."

To illustrate my point, I slide my finger into the elastic waistband of his boxers and work my hold around to his hips. I tug them down, stopping briefly to pull the fabric out and over the head of his cock.

He lifts his hips and I'm good to shove the cloth barrier down his chiseled thighs and out of my way.

Dune doesn't seem to be in half the hurry I'm in.

He peels the sides of my underwear down my leg and then slides his fingers into the space he made.

"The other time there was a crowd," he says, rubbing his nose against my cheek. "I didn't get to take my time. Do you mind?"

I read the sincerity in his gaze and draw a lazy breath. He's trying. I asked him to start taking this seriously and try harder and he's doing that.

"Take all the time you need."

His grin is the reward that tells me I nailed that one. He finishes stripping off my underwear and then rubs the silk and lace over his cheek and across his mouth. "I love your scent."

Before it gets weird and I have to think of an answer to that, he rolls over me and props up on his elbows. "Open your legs for me, beautiful."

His command comes out with more need than demand and my knees fall open at an embarrassing rate.

I refuse to think about it. Warm kisses trail up the line of my jaw to the tender flesh behind my ear. All the while, he rolls his hips, spreading the moisture he's waking in me and slicking the cock probing at my core.

I trail my hands over the contours of his back, memorizing the muscles and scars. Unlike my faery wings, his wings don't retract. They're massive and heavy and oh, so sexy.

They're also incredibly soft to the touch.

As I raise my hands to stroke the sandy brown plumage, he opens them above us to give me better access. "Are the spinal ridges for your wings an erogenous zone for you like they are for me?"

I run my fingers along the strong protrusions from his back and stroke the cartilage there.

"Oh, yeah." Dune's hips thrust forward, and the penetration is breathtaking. His morning erection is hot and hard and we fit together beautifully.

My head tilts back as I stretch around him. "Oh, that feels wonderful. Unintentional or not, I'm glad we're here and doing this."

"I've been crazy for days. With the magic of our union, I've needed to fill you. I'm sorry it took me so long to be worthy of being inside you." He presses deep inside me and stills. His eyes roll closed as a gentle smile softens his expression. "I never want to leave this bed."

"Oh... I like this side of you."

He starts to move, and I rake my fingers across his back urging the rock and glide to continue. The beauty of enacting the union of bonding with warriors is that I never have to worry that they'll tire out.

Warriors are fit and healthy and strong and they crave their female.

Dune can keep this up for as long as I need.

And oh boy do I need.

"I enjoyed your dirty text last night, Princess," he says, nipping my jaw. His tongue is warm and wet as he brushes over the sting of his gentle bite. "My answer is yes. Name the time and place. I'll bring the supplies."

Supplies? What supplies? What text?

I don't want to start a conversation at the moment. I just want to be here being thoroughly filled. "Kiss me."

Dune's smile widens and he bends to claim my mouth. His lips are warm and silky as they glide over mine. His kiss is playful, but not with the same cocky edge he used when we got together as a group.

I have a feeling I'm getting my first glimpse of the real Dune. With his elbows pressing into the mattress beside my ribs, he hooks his hands under my shoulders to leverage his thrusts.

I groan, absorbing the bliss of being filled by him. The union is taking hold. I feel the connection between us growing. This is more than morning sex to him.

This is him showing me what's behind all those walls he puts up. This is him being vulnerable to me.

Gods, you gotta love a guy who lets you see his soft and gooey insides.

He eases back from our kiss, picking up speed on the slide and glide of in and out. His rhythm is perfect, each stroke stronger and deeper than the last.

I lift my feet off the mattress and hook my heels around the back of his muscled thighs. The shift in position opens me wider and gives his hips even more room to move.

"You're so beautiful," he breaths, his gaze hauntingly intimate. "Too good for me by every measure. I'll make myself worthy, Princess. I swear it."

I hear the pain and insecurity lacing his words, but now is not the time to argue his suitability to be in my life. My mind is abuzz, and my release is building. "Keep doing what you're doing and we'll both be fine."

More than fine.

He pushes up onto his palms and his thrusts grow stronger, faster. "Tell me I get to come inside you like this for the rest of my life."

"As often as you want."

Hooking his elbows under my knees, he pushes forward, pinning me open to his penetrations. Pleasure vibrates through me and I reach behind my head, pressing my palms against the wall to brace myself before I ride up the bed behind the thundering thrusts.

The sound of flesh slapping flesh... of my throaty gasps... of the bed frame banging against the wall.

I close my eyes and let the ebbing throb of my pussy take hold. It pulls inside me. Building. Aching. Keening.

My release hits fast and my body quakes, convulsing in heated waves of pleasure. My inner muscles grip and pulse, milking Dune.

"Don't stop," I gasp, throbbing around him as I grip his shoulders. "So good."

His breath escapes in throaty bursts and then his rhythm falters. He slams his hips forward and stiffens.

I study his face as his release hits,

He spills into me, the twisted torture of his orgasm racking him in agonized beauty.

After a few pounding heartbeats, he opens his eyes and meets my gaze. We stay like that until he relaxes and drops back to his elbows again. "Do you mind if I never want to pull out of you?"

I chuckle. "It'll make going to the castle a little more difficult."

He drops his mouth to my collarbone, his breath warm against my flesh. "I suppose that's true."

"This was lovely." I run my fingers through his sandy brown hair and then hug him. "Thank you."

He eases out from between my thighs and I miss him immediately. "Anytime. I mean it. Anytime. Anyplace. Any urge you need sated. Tell me and I am yours."

I roll to my side to face him. "I look forward to the next time."

I give him a soft kiss, climb over him and grab my undies off the corner of the bed. On the way to the washroom to clean up, I find my pants discarded on the floor. After scooping them up too, I look both ways in the hall before padding over to the barrack washrooms.

Hopefully, the Guardian's suite has a private bathroom. I have a feeling that with three men in my bed, I'm going to need one close by.

~

Tundra

"You can stop pretending to be asleep now."

I open my eyes and prop my head on my hand. "I was giving the two of you a private moment."

I brace myself for a snarky comeback, but Dune surprises me. "Thank you. That was thoughtful. It was a wonderful moment."

What's this? A real moment with Dune?

Color me astonished.

When Honor asked me to go find Lukas yesterday afternoon, she wasn't pleased with him. They must've had a serious heart-to-heart.

I'm glad.

It seems she got through to him.

At least for the moment.

The two of us are lying in opposite directions on the mattress. With him being naked, it's impossible for me not to notice him. Thankfully, I've got the sheet draped across my hips so he can't see how turned on their lovemaking made me. "You're wrong, though."

"Oh? Wrong about what?"

"You *are* worthy of her and of being here. You just have to own it and rise to your potential."

He raises his face to the ceiling and closes his eyes.

I wait for a few minutes and when he doesn't say anything more, I assume he's fallen back to sleep. Rolling off the bed, I grab my pants and head down the hall to piss and start my day.

I only get as far as the doorway when—

"Thanks, T," Dune says. "I appreciate you saying so. I hope you're right."

Twice in one conversation? Wow, that must've been one hell of a pep talk.

"I am. Put in the effort and you'll see."

Leaving him to think about things, I head into the washroom and toss my clothes on the long, ten-person sink. Stepping up to the urinal, I take a deep breath and wait for my erection to ease enough that I can piss.

One of the showers is on deeper in the room and I envision Honor under the spray, her body glistening as hot water beads down her breasts... her ribs... the bare flesh of her mound.

I glare down at my stiff cock.

Okay, thoughts like that aren't helping.

A feminine song drifts along with the hiss of shower spray and I close my eyes and smile. She's singing. I make a mental note to be extra nice to Dune today. He did good. He sated her need, and our princess is happy.

Point to him.

I manage to finish off before my thoughts drift back to the two of them having sex. It's a good thing too because the moment I flush and head over to the sink to wash my hands, things are already getting hard again.

At the sound of the hand towels being pulled, Honor stops singing.

"It's only me, Princess. Don't let me stop you from your song. Do you mind if I take a shower as well?"

"Do you mean with me or in your own stall?"

I chuckle, my cock quick to respond to the invitation. "I meant in my own stall. While I would love to share a shower with you, there is much to do today."

"There is. Raincheck then."

"Definitely." I step into one of the showers on the opposite side of the aisle from hers and turn the faucet on. The water starts off cold and that's a good thing, it will help my body discard its last hopes of a sexual start to my day.

After a couple of minutes under the spray, I curse at what's happening below my navel. I don't have time for every thought and every interaction to devolve into sex.

Except... I won't get anything done sporting a stone shaft all day.

But stroking myself to completion with Honor showering across the hall seems disrespectful.

I shut the water off and decide to take this show on the road. Maybe if I—

"Is everything all right, Tundra?" Honor asks as I step out of the stall and stride toward the towel shelf.

"Fine, Princess. I, uh... just remembered something that needs doing."

She steps out, glistening wet and her eyes shift straight down to where my towel is being poked well out from my waist. "Something that needs doing, you say?"

I roll my eyes. "I'm sorry, Princess. Between waking up with you and Dune sharing a moment, and then talking with Dune after, and then you being in here showering... I'll regain control of things, I swear. At the moment, though, my body seems to be responding to all the union stimuli as if I'm a teenager again."

She chuckles. "There's no shame in being hungry for what this group offers."

"No, but there is a time and place."

"True, but as you said, you don't have complete control over what's happening right now."

"I'm a grown man. I can handle things quickly and without drawing you into it. Don't give it another thought."

"If that's the way you want to handle it, fine, but I have a better idea."

I close my eyes. "What idea is that?"

"Let me help you shower. We'll be quick. We won't hold up the day or get carried away, just me helping you blow off some sexual tension before our day."

I bark a laugh. "You don't need to..."

She drops her towel. "Nothing fancy. Just join me for five minutes and I'll have you bathed and ready to face our day. What's five minutes? Nothing. Come on. Let me suds you up and ease you. We won't get carried away. It'll be so not sexy it'll be clinical."

I laugh. "I doubt that very much."

"Okay, maybe not, but I want to be part of easing you. I insist."

I laugh again. "Very well. If you insist."

CHAPTER ELEVEN

Shadow

I wake to the scent of bacon and the incessant throbbing of my brain trying to force itself free from my skull.

"Morning, sunshine," Lukas says, across from me.

"Why did I think pounding back alcohol like it's college frosh was a good idea?"

"Because night guy is an asshole and never cares how badly he's screwing over morning guy."

I try to lift my head but then decide it weighs too much and I will be stuck on this couch for the rest of my long, elven life. "Might you have a magical remedy to alleviate the migration of my gray matter out my ears?"

The deep chuckle that follows is sexy and seductive. "I think I can help you out. Here. Drink this."

I hold out my hands and he wraps my fingers around the handle of a warm mug.

"It's a family recipe to cure what ails you. Go ahead. I promise you'll feel better once you get it down."

The way he says that I expect it to be a foul concoction. It's not. It tastes like warm cider and sunshine. I take a few sips to test how receptive my stomach is to the influx of more fluid and surprisingly, my body seems quite welcoming of the idea.

"Gratitude. It is very good."

"It's actually horrible, but I spelled it with a bit of extra love to take the edge off."

"Much appreciated." I sip at the smooth, ceramic edge for a few more minutes before my mind comes back online. "Am I the last to get up?"

"Maybe, but the other three haven't come down yet. I heard the water running about five minutes ago, so I started cooking. Bacon sandwich?"

The idea of eating bacon right now sounds horrible in theory, but not half bad in practice. "Let me try. If the gods are with me, it will stay down."

"I'll be right back. Keep drinking your remedy."

I do. With every sip, my head hurts less, and the angry eels playing chase around in my stomach settle down another notch.

"Here you go. I'll trade you, a mug for a plate."

We make the exchange and when the couch beside me dips, I shift so I can eat my sandwich and not be facing in the wrong direction. "Did you sleep down here?"

"Yeah. I'm an early riser and wanted to check in with Rhylan first thing. I took one of the other couches and got up a few hours ago."

I take a bite of my toasted sandwich. It is buttery and has cheese and bacon. It is quite good. "You don't need to babysit me. I might be new to the void of
sightlessness, but I shall make do."

"I have no doubt you will, but I wasn't babysitting you. I feel like I've been monopolizing Honor's affections and it's causing tension with Dune. She told me yesterday that she gave him a solid dressing down and he promised to try harder. Considering he and I haven't found common ground yet, I figured I'd hang out with you down here and give them some private time."

"That is generous and mature of you."

"Not my first rodeo, my friend."

"Speaking of things not being your first. You never did answer my question about your elven lover." I take another bite of my sandwich and chew, waiting eagerly to hear how he answers.

"And this stays between us?"

I swallow. "Of course."

"I spent time with two lady's maids for a very prominent elven family of nobility. It would tarnish their standing in their community if it became known that they slept with a human."

"I imagine it would. Some of the demands on nobility are backward and out of date."

"True story. So, during the course of Hawk establishing the Fae Counsel, he had numerous meetings within their woodland community. I accompanied him for the meetings and the elves were very welcoming. The three of us shared memorable moments and I consider them a dear and cherished part of my past."

The tension in his voice is obvious.

"Your liaison is safe with me."

"Thank you."

I swallow another bite of my sandwich and swallow. "If telling me your truths made you so uncomfortable, why did you confide in me?"

"It's not so much about telling my truths, I value my honor. I don't speak about private issues involving others lightly."

"And yet you answered my question."

"I did." The soft brush of his plate on the surface of the coffee table precedes a long silence. "Last night, after the others went to bed, I laid on the couch and watched you sleep." He chuckles. "Sorry, that sounded much creepier in words than it did in my head."

"Not to worry. I am not creeped out in the slightest."

"Good." He shifts beside me. "As simple as it would be to say that the kiss we shared was a drunken moment, the connection I felt seemed like more. I meant it when I said I noticed you. Those weeks we spent taking care of Honor made an impression on me."

"For me as well."

"At the time, I was distracted by my attraction to Honor. Spending time with her—connected to her—it altered something inside me. It was more than infatuation. I bonded with her."

I finish with my plate and brush away the crumbs from my fingertips. "I am pleased for you, truly, but what does this have to do with you watching me sleep?"

"Things with Honor and I heated up and I thought life was good but then you got hurt. I visited you more than once. Did you know that?"

"No."

"Well, I did. I sat there, watching you lay unconscious and the pressure in my chest was agonizing. We hadn't shared anything beyond a polite companionship, so why did it hit me so hard? At the time, I thought it was because I was driving the truck. Now I don't think that was it after all."

One of the first things you learn as a counselor is that some people need to talk through what brought them to the present. The speaking of events can open self-discovery. It feels like that is what Lukas is doing.

I turn on the seat and shift until my knee touches his. "Tell me, how did you feel sitting at my bedside?"

"I was sad, of course. I felt the guilt of being the driver of the truck when you were hurt. And I was worried about why you weren't waking up."

"Sorrow, guilt, worry... anything else?"

"Yeah. More than all of those, I felt an ebbing loss... and not the kind of loss I normally feel when something bad happens."

A gentle brush across my jaw takes his caress to the shell of my ear. I tilt my head into his palm and close my eyes. "What kind of loss?"

"It was... my heart ached with the loss of opportunity. You're more than a good guy sharing the same circle of friends. When Doc didn't know if you'd ever wake up, all I could think of was maybe Honor wasn't the only one I bonded to during those weeks..."

His thumb brushes over the sensitive tip of my ear. His caress massages the flesh of the peak, and the contact quickens my pulse. It sends a zing of need straight to my groin and my cock stirs with arousal.

Damn. He knows what that does to an elf.

What does it mean that he's touching me so intimately like this a second time?

And this time, not under the influence of alcohol.

Lukas shifts on the couch and urges me closer. Tugging me forward, he leans in. The warmth of his breath tingles against my cheek. "Shadow... I—"

The squeal of Honor's laughter interrupts Lukas's thoughts. He whispers a low oath against my lips and then pulls away.

I want to stand and beg him to finish. I want the kiss he was about to give me... but the moment is broken.

Lukas

Fuck me. Seriously. Fuck my life. I rub my sweaty palms down my thighs and put enough distance between me and Shadow to not cause a scene. I was two seconds away from pouring my heart out and claiming the elf's kiss for a second time.

Dammit. What was I thinking? I'm already in a four-way relationship that's just getting off the ground. Why would I complicate his life or ours by wanting more? Am I that greedy?

"There's our fearless magic man," Honor says, dropping to her bare feet in the grand entrance, her wings fluttering behind her. "Looking good, babe."

As I greet her, she runs her hand down the front of my body and gives my sac a gentle squeeze. "You three are in a good mood."

"Eager to start our day."

Dune and Tundra are all grins as they fold their wings back and I give them a knowing nod. Good. It seems my stepping back gave them some much-needed Honor alone time.

"You do realize that no matter how eager you are to start your day, the stairs serve a purpose."

Honor grins. "Wings are faster and much more fun."

"And stunning." I claim her hand and press it against the front of my pants. "Don't forget stunning."

"You likey?"

I laugh at the sass. "Very much. Now, if the three of you are finished lounging away the morning, it's time for us to get to work. Today's a big day."

"A big day how?" Tundra asks.

I hike my thumb over my shoulder and lead them back into the community room. "I set the things we talked about last night into motion. Rhylan has a press event scheduled for later this morning to announce the call for Amberloq applicants."

Honor laughs. "Excellent, but we were drunk. I can't even remember the details of how we're running the qualification tournament."

"I thought of that. Rhylan and Creed are looking over the criteria we came up with and will suggest any changes or additions before the press event."

"Good thinking. All right, then what?"

"Hawk is loaning me the helicopter so we can go to the forested jungle biome after lunch. I realize the three of you have wings, but I don't. This way we can all fly."

"I'm not riding in that metal pea pod," Dune snaps. "I'll fly thanks."

"Suit yourself, just remember to stay tight to the spinning blades. They're good for a close shave."

Dune scowls but I don't give a shit—that was funny.

Honor thinks so too.

She chuckles and waves her hand to stop the volley of snark I'm expecting. "All right. No bickering. We're trying something new today—it's called getting along."

I dip my chin. "We can certainly try."

She seems to appreciate my acquiescence. "So, we go over the tournament with Creed, then the press event, and then a trip to the Elbirfae forest. Is that it?"

"No. Then we come back, and you spend time in your secret lair listening to your discs. Ruic Breard and his rich, asshole friends are coming for the crown. We need to bust our butts to stop them at every turn."

"And what are we doing while Honor studies the discs?" Tundra asks.

"We're working on the currency situation. We need to figure out a viable solution to Ruic holding the Dornte economy in his crooked fingers. As long as he has control of the money, Dornte is in jeopardy."

"I might have an idea about that," Shadow says, sitting straighter on the couch. "I was thinking about the EU and how when they—"

His words choke off and a hot surge of magic spikes in the

air. The hair on my body stands on end and by the looks in the group, I'm not the only one.

"Shadow? Are you okay?" I rush around the coffee table and kneel on the carpet before him. "What's happening? One of you, call Doc. Something's wrong."

Shadow's blank, white eyes burst into a golden glow as his hair lifts and writhes straight out from his skull like he's some kind of purple-haired Medusa.

"That is officially horrifying," Dune says, hightailing it for the doorway. "Anyone else need a coffee?"

Words rip from Shadow's throat, his voice not close to being his own...

The child of fire, the moon of light,
A sea of blood to stain the night,
The foe of freedom, the king is down,
A war of outcasts to hold the crown.

I'm frozen in front of him but when his body goes limp and slumps to the side, I ease him over. Tundra sweeps his legs up for him to lay down.

"Hand me that—" I point to the blanket.

Honor grabs it and hurries in to make him more comfortable. I've got my fingers on his throat, trying to make sense of his pulse. "Fuck, his heart is racing."

"His skin is cold and clammy."

"We called Doc, yeah?"

Honor nods. "I did. They're on the way."

"What the hell just happened?" I ask, wholly unprepared for any of this.

"I think Keyla and Doc know. They alluded to something important and private about Shadow's condition and encouraged me to get him to open up."

"Did you?"

"No. He wanted to get drunk, so I didn't push. But before they left, they said if anything concerning should happen, we should call them."

"Concerning?" I blink, my heart racing almost as out of control as Shadow's. "I'd say that Exorcist routine was pretty fucking concerning."

"Yep. I'm pretty sure that's what they meant." Honor leans over me and hugs me from above. "Oh, babe, you're trembling. Are you okay? I've never known you to get the shakes when a crisis hits."

Now is not the time to tell her that Shadow is under my skin. "I'm fine. And I'll be a lot finer once Doc gets here. The walk through the forest takes too fucking long. I'm buying dirt bikes. Put that on the list."

Honor's soft chuckle is a balm to my soul. It eases me away from the edge of the cliff. "He'll be all right. Doc seemed concerned but not worried. We'll know more in a few minutes."

"I can tell you right now," Tundra says.

I crank my head and peg him with a glare. "You know what that was?"

"I do. I also know what he is."

What he *is?* "What the fuck does that mean?"

"He's an oracle. I saw an episode once before when one came to speak to Valorous. They are incredibly rare and I didn't realize the Human Realm even had any, but I'm quite sure. The woman who came to meet with your aunt had an episode and her message affected her exactly as Shadow's did him."

Message? "Shit. I wasn't paying attention to what was said. Did either of you catch it?"

Tundra nods. "I recorded it on my tablet. We can revisit it once everything calms down."

"Oh, good work, Tundra," Honor says. "Quick thinking on your part."

The knock on the front door is frantic. I can relate. Tundra strides off to let Doc in and I fight to breathe.

Damn. I really am a mess. Ha! I guess I owe Hawk two beers now... or maybe a keg.

~

Dune

Slecking hell... Shadow's an oracle. And the day started out so well. I leave the others to figure things out and take a straight path to the kitchen. This development makes it even more important to get our day started.

If word gets out that there is an oracle in Dornte... slecking hell. No matter how much it hurts my pride to admit it, we're not ready to take on the wave of trouble that will bring.

"Hey? Are you all right?" Honor joins me in the massive stainless steel and white tile room. "You cleared out pretty quick."

"I know he's your friend, but he can't stay. When the wizarding families find out there's an oracle beyond the veil of ancient Aramos, they will come for him."

"Then we keep it quiet."

"Keep it quiet? Did you miss the freakshow of what happened out there? If he's speaking with someone in the castle or when the trainees get here or anywhere near you or your brother when he has one of those spells, our job to protect the crown gets a hundred times more complicated."

"Let's not hit the eject button just yet. That was the first episode he ever suffered. Maybe it was a one-off."

I frown. "You don't believe that. Obviously whatever went wrong after the accident jarred something loose in him and now he needs to get gone."

"Shadow's not going anywhere," Lukas snaps, striding into the kitchen. "And if you talk about getting rid of him like he's dog shit on your shoe again, it'll be you that's gone."

"Says the man who has no business being here in the first place. This is Amberloq business, human. Take your elf crush and leave."

My feathers ruffle with the influx of magic and raise my arms to block my face from a dozen pots and frying pans rocketing through the air. The metal clang and bang has me ducking but I catch the blur of his attack as he closes in.

The fist that connects with my face hits like a block of concrete. My head snaps back as magic shorts out my synapsis. My ass hits the tile before I have a chance to regroup and then I'm seeing spots.

I must've passed out because when I blink back to reality Honor is blocking Lukas and my face is throbbing like it has a life of its own.

"Stay the fuck away from me, birdman. If you know what's good for you, you'll steer clear of me."

When he turns on his heels and storms out of the kitchen, I let out a long breath. "Good riddance."

"Good riddance?" Honor snaps, looking dazzled. "Lukas isn't going anywhere and neither is Shadow. What's wrong with you?"

"Me? Other than your boyfriend smashing my face for no good reason, nothing's wrong with me."

"Except that you're utterly self-absorbed. I don't know how your nomadic community handled trouble but, in my world, and in my home, when someone is in trouble you close ranks and protect them, you don't boot them out the door."

"But having Shadow here puts everyone at risk."

"And having me here does too. If you recall, there is an army of rebels out to kill me. And then there's my brother. Should we kick the king to the curb too because rebels are intent on bringing chaos to his reign?"

I curse. "Of course not. You and your brother belong here. You're from here. They're from the Human Realm. Why should we risk the success of our destiny on people who don't count."

"Everyone counts," Honor says, deflating. "Why can't you understand that? You need to stop judging people as unwelcome simply because they look different than you and come from a faraway land. What matters is who they are inside and what they stand for."

"Princess," Tundra says, frowning as he jogs into the room. "Shadow's awake and asking for you."

Honor starts for the door before turning back to pierce me with a ball-shriveling glare. "The man I woke up with this morning is welcome to stay and work this out. If he wasn't real, I'm sorry to say, you should go. We have enough to work out without fighting amongst ourselves."

My breath locks in my chest as she turns her back on me. "Seriously? She's choosing them over me? *I'm* her Amberloq General."

Tundra shakes his head. "You still don't get it. Respect and status are earned. Lukas proves himself an asset a hundred times every day. Shadow has served the Wolf Queen, the people of Dornte, and Honor with his whole heart since he arrived here. They earned their place by their actions and expect nothing in return."

"And what? I've been sitting on my ass? Is that what you're saying?"

"What are your contributions? What have you done without vying for something in return? Honor said you're self-absorbed, and you are, but she hasn't known you as long as I have. It's entitlement. You actually believe the world owes you simply for being you."

"No, I don't."

"Yes, you do. You're ruining this, Dune. *You.* And yet you point fingers and insult and judge and refuse to acknowledge it."

Before I have a chance to respond to that, he turns and walks out.

I'm not ruining this. I'm the only one who's seeing things clearly. They'll see.

CHAPTER TWELVE

Honor

*L*ukas, Keyla, and Doc help Shadow up to the second bedroom in the master suite while Creed, Tundra, and I go over the details of how we're going to handle the Amberloq tournament. Our address to the citizens is in a few hours and we need to know what we're promoting to the people. "And you think this will work?"

Creed looks to Keyla and then nods. "It's not dissimilar to something Keyla's family sets up in the Human Realm. I think between lowering the age requirement, the strict vetting, and applicants being questioned in the presence of Keyla and/or Kotah, we'll be able to select the strongest candidates and weed out any potential threats trying to get on the inside of things."

"Rhylan is working on the vetting questions now," Keyla says. "Between our heightened sense of smell and sensitivity to emotions, we should be able to keep any rebel troublemakers out of our ranks."

"Is it realistic to think we'll be able to keep them out altogether?" Tundra asks.

Creed shakes his head. "Likely not, but it's a start."

Tundra straightens before me and clasps his hands at his back. "If you put your faith in me, I will volunteer to oversee the tournament details and the building of the Amberloq numbers. Having been a warrior within the organization for almost a decade, it's a topic on our long list of things to do where I feel I can be effective."

I extend my reach and take his hand. "Yes, of course. I love that idea and have total confidence in you. Thank you for stepping up."

He nods. "To that end, I suggest Lukas stay here and work on tracking down Ruic and the guns. Dune and I can fly to the Forested Jungle Biome and assess what happened with the third General. Also, you might find your time better spent by staying here to study the Guardian Chronicles."

I hear the wisdom in his words even though I'd like to go with them. He's right. Time to divide and conquer.

"I look forward to hearing what you find. Also, I want to be kept informed on progress and any problems with the tournament. I have every confidence you can get things off the ground, but I want to remain involved."

"Of course."

Lukas jogs into the room and I meet him with a hug. "You look tired, magic man. Did you get any sleep on the couch last night?"

He smiles down at me, and I see the answer in the purple bags beneath his eyes. "I'll nap on the helicopter later."

"We've changed that plan," I say, gesturing to Tundra. "We've decided that you and I will stay and Dune and Tundra will check in with the forest biome."

The worry lines beside his eyes tighten. "Are you sure?"

"Positive. I'll do the press announcement with Creed, and then come back and spend the afternoon in my library going through discs. That frees you up to work with Rhylan tracking down Ruic and the guns smuggled into the quadrant."

He doesn't look thrilled, but he doesn't argue. "If I'm at the castle and Dune and Tundra are gone, I want you to promise you'll stay inside."

I lean up onto my toes and brush his lips with mine. "I promise. If Doc can stay with Shadow for a bit now, I can relieve him once I'm back."

Lukas gives in and raises his fist to bump with Tundra. "I guess we'll see you later. Good luck."

"Thank you. I'll collect Dune and be back as soon as possible. Be safe, both of you."

~

Lukas

The walk back to the castle an hour later is a quiet one. I'm exhausted—both physically and emotionally—and have way too much on my mind.

"You can lean on me too," Honor says, smiling over at me as we reach the main path. "I know you're usually the strong one and I'm the one spilling, but it goes both ways."

I lace my fingers with hers and squeeze. "I appreciate that."

"But you're not going to tell me what's going on with you?"

"There's too much to make sense of. It's all a jumble right now. I'll figure it out."

"I have no doubt you will, but as your lover, I'd like to help you, if I can."

We walk in silence a while longer and I negotiate with myself over what I should and shouldn't tell her. "I think splitting up to get more done was a good call. There are a lot of issues looming—your safety, the goblins, the Amberloq, the four of us... and now Shadow."

"Why do I get the feeling there is more to the Shadow issue than him being an oracle?"

I brush my thumb over the back of her hand. "That transparent, am I?"

"It's obvious to anyone in the room with you two. There's something there."

I stop walking and face her. "I'm sorry about that. I feel like I've let you down. I fucked up and I don't know how to fix it."

Her expression sobers. "Fucked up how?"

"This morning, while you three were still upstairs, Shadow and I were having a heart-to-heart, and I... I got swept up in the moment."

She swallows, her shoulders straightening. "What did you do?"

"I almost kissed him. Honestly, it wasn't even an almost. If you three hadn't come downstairs when you did, I would've kissed him. I'm so sorry."

"Why are you torturing yourself over an almost kiss? There is a lot of emotion surrounding Shadow right now and the two of you obviously care about one another—"

"I don't want you to think... I mean... I am one hundred percent in love with you. There's no doubt in my mind about that. I'm in this with you until the end. I'm trying with Dune and Tundra and we're getting there, but I'm developing those relationships for you."

"I realize that," she says, her tone cautious.

"But if I'm being honest... Shadow was already under my skin. I know that sounds greedy. Here I have this incredible female and her two companions and I'm fumbling over feelings for someone else. I didn't mean for it to happen. I don't even know if he feels the same way. I'm sorry. It shouldn't matter."

"Of course it should. You and I have something truly special." She presses her hand to my chest and taps her fingers over my heart. "You're in here. I feel you connected to my soul. I know your heart and intentions. I don't think you're greedy. Shadow is an exceptional person. I'm not a bit surprised you have feelings for him."

"How can you not be? *I* am. I didn't expect my reaction to that kiss last night. I was blown away."

"Sometimes love is a conscious choice to nurture feelings. Sometimes it's a lightning strike. When you and Shadow shared that kiss last night, it was definitely a lightning strike."

I run my hand under her hair and caress her neck. "I'm sorry to complicate things."

She chuckles, her stunning purple gaze glittering with amusement. "Everything we're dealing with is complicated. I'd say your feelings for me and for Shadow are the least complicated thing on the list. Don't be sorry. You're acting like you betrayed me somehow for having feelings for him."

"Because that's how I feel."

"Well don't. That's not how I feel."

I search her gaze, my mind spinning. "What do you want me to do about my attraction to Shadow? Do I bury it? Do I bring it up with him? With all the other things coming at us at the moment, I'm lost. I don't want to fuck up anything with you or Tundra or Dune. The three of you have to solidify to get your destiny back on track. I won't be the cause of turmoil."

She reaches over my shoulders and links her fingers behind my neck. "There's no turmoil. You don't bury it. Shadow's a great guy. He's caring and smart and I was speaking to Keyla while you were upstairs getting him settled. His Elven family won't accept him as an oracle and the oracles won't accept him after living in modern society his entire life. He is truly alone in this."

Even thinking that makes my chest ache.

I can't imagine going through something so life-altering and realizing there is no one willing to stand behind you. "That kills me."

"Me too," she says. "He's not alone. We'll make him part of our family whether or not you and he have a future. I want you to do what you need to do today with Rhylan but then go back to the hall and spend time with him. No expectations. No recriminations. Just see where the two of you are."

"You're sure?" My heart is beating so heavy in my chest I can barely breathe.

"Of course I'm sure. There's no wrong answer here except denying it and hurting both of you. Be honest with him and yourself. See where that takes you."

I wrap my arms around her and pull her against my chest. Claiming her mouth has become second nature. I'm more comfortable holding her and kissing her than I've ever been with anyone else in my lifetime.

The minty freshness of her lips makes me smile and suddenly, I don't feel so tired and overwhelmed anymore. When I end the kiss, I draw a deep breath into my lungs and press my forehead to hers. "I love you Honor Thornebane. I love you to the depth of my soul."

She grins up at me and runs her hands down the muscles of my arms. "You better. I plan on spending the rest of my life with you."

"Done deal."

Turning her toward the castle, I wrap my arm around her back and pull her against my side. Yeah, I could get used to a lifetime of this.

Tundra

Dune and I leave for the forested section of Dornte immediately after I find him in the kitchen of Amberloq Hall. He was still sulking about the three of us being judgmental and rude to him and I realize, he may never see what's right in front of his face.

He has the most incredible life opportunity awaiting him. All he has to do to make it a reality is step up and be the man I know he could be.

The Amberloq bar is raised above the rest.

There are standards and restrictions to being a Guardian General. That's because there is a great meaning behind the position and importance to the success of the entire quadrant.

It's not a title he won in the aftermath of evil queen genocide. He doesn't just get to collect his prize and sail through life.

He doesn't see that.

I don't know how to make him see that.

"You're quiet," Dune says, rolling in the air to glide beside me on his back. "Is this the way it's going to be now? The three of you punching me and then not talking to me?"

"I honestly don't know what to say to you anymore, Dune. You don't listen. Everything anyone says falls on deaf ears and makes no difference."

He frowns and rolls back to fly properly. "Or maybe I hear you, but I don't agree. Everyone is always judging me. Maybe if people took a moment to see what I do offer instead of what I don't they'd see I'm not such a waste of oxygen."

"I have never, *ever*, thought you were a waste of oxygen but you see and hear what you think regardless."

"So, it's all on me, is it? Of course, it is."

I sigh and check the GPS on my tactical watch. "The very last thing I'll say on the matter is this. At some point, when you're sitting alone in a room and your mind is quiet, lower your guard and try to see what we've been saying from our point of view. Step outside yourself and look at things from another perspective."

"And you think if I do that, I'll have an epiphany and be all like, damn, they're right. It *is* all me. I'm a worthless piece of shit."

I align my internal compass and adjust our course.

"No one thinks that. You are a brave, skilled, and talented warrior. I'd never say or allow anyone else to say anything to the contrary. You're just not a nice person to be around."

"I'm nice."

I won't argue the matter. It wouldn't make any difference if I did. I don't know what it'll take to make him see his flaws but it's not anything I say. If it were, he would've seen them already.

"The forest biome capitol building is below. On your guard. We don't know what we'll find down there."

I tuck back my wings and dive toward the canopy of the forest below. Wind whistles past my face and I spot a break in the overlapping foliage of two large trees.

I take the lead, and for once in his life, Dune takes the rear without objection.

When we land, I scan the crumbled front steps of a massive jungle ruin. "This was once the business center for this biome."

The stone building lays in uneven heaps of rubble with animals scurrying into holes in the walls and over the skeletons of fallen Elbirfae.

"What the slecking hell happened here?" Dune asks, taking in the desolation and destruction.

"I have no idea but based on the overgrowth and the stage of bodily decomposition, it happened some time ago—years maybe."

Dune frowns. "I guess this explains why no General of the Forest Biome answered the call to serve Honor."

"Do you think the entire species is gone?"

"Gone, yes. Whether that means dead and extinct... I have no idea."

My breath feels heavy in my lungs. "Fan out and have a good look around before we return. Take note of anything that tells us what happened or who did this. We'll meet back here in twenty minutes."

Dune checks his watch and nods. "Twenty minutes."

❧

Shadow

The child of fire, the moon of light,
A sea of blood to stain the night,
The foe of freedom, the king is down,
A war of outcasts to hold the crown.

I listen to the replay of the video in horror. And, as the first prophecy as a cursed oracle tears from my throat, I realize there is no going back. This is my future. "Sweet mercies. Is it as horrifying to see as it sounds?"

Keyla sighs and eases the phone out of my hand. "I'll admit, it's alarming to watch but it's not something you can control. As well, the Ordained have been responsible for some of the most important political, military, and humanitarian saves in our world. Let's not forget that."

"Keyla's right," Doc says over by the exit. "There's no helping the fact that your recessive genetics have activated. This is the new you. Let's get past the unnerving part of it and talk about what's important."

"If you give me a speech about being alive and healthy, I will have to bodily harm you."

Doc chuckles. "Then it's good that isn't what I'm saying. My point is that a prophecy was given. Let's get our minds off the delivery and focus on the message."

I run my hand over the blanket across my lap and frown. "I could focus better if I weren't laying on this bed with the two of you looking at me like I am a psychiatric patient."

"You're blind," Doc says, "so, in truth, you have no idea how we're looking at you, but your point is valid. Let's go down to the community room, grab a couple of drinks, and then wander the hedge maze for a bit."

"That's a great idea," Keyla says. "What do you say, Shadow?"

I shrug. "It is better than staying here."

The three of us make our way out of the Guardian's master suite and down to the back porch. When Doc emerges, I hear the glass of bottles jingling together, and then the three of us stride off toward the labyrinth maze.

Well, striding off might be giving too much credit.

The breeze is blocked and the sounds of the forest surrounding the Amberloq mansion quiet down as we step into the opening of the maze.

"All right, let's get this party started." Doc uncaps three bottles, hands them out. "Creed told me he and Honor used to roam this maze for hours trying to find the hidden treasure."

I take a long swig of ale and let the chill of the alcohol work its wonders. "Is there a real treasure within or an urban legend told to keep children busy?"

Keyla squeezes my arm. "I asked the same question. They never figured that out."

"Good story."

Keyla chuckles. "Whether or not there is gold and diamonds hidden here or just the treasure of spending time with friends, it's a lovely escape from the norm."

Doc's footsteps are heavy against the grass and twigs and I track his movement at my side. "Creed says there's a fountain at the center."

Keyla's footsteps are almost inaudible. She moves through nature with the grace of an elf. "Kotah and I explored the outer rings but that's as far as we got."

I finish my first beer and exchange the bottle for a second. "So, what do you think the prophecy means?"

Doc sighs. "I think the first bit is easy enough. *The child of fire, the moon of light, a sea of blood to stain the night.* I'd say that's about the coming of our phoenix baby and a big bad something accompanying her birth."

"I hate to think about that," Keyla says, "but I agree. It sounds like she'll be born on the night of the full moon and that there will be bloodshed."

"The full moon?" I ask.

"The moon of light," she says. "The light moon is a wildling term for the full moon."

"So, the young one is coming on the full moon and then there is a sea of bloodshed." I curse and press the bottle to my lips, swallowing another long drink. "May I just say, I hate everything about this."

Keyla squeezes my arm. "Don't look at it like that. Maybe you having a premonition will allow us to prepare and save lives. This could be a good thing."

"Exactly," Doc says. "The question is, since Dornte has two moons, which full moon are we talking about and when will that be?"

"And is it the next full moon or just 'a' full moon?" Keyla asks. "No one seems to know what the gestation period for a baby phoenix is."

"All good questions," Doc says. "So, moving on from there... *The foe of freedom, the king is down, A war of outcasts to hold the crown.* I think your prophecy is a head's up for us to rally the outcasts to be ready for an attack. This could be a good thing."

"I wish I saw it that way."

"Maybe you will one day," Keyla says. "It's still new. Don't let self-loathing pull you under just yet."

I sigh. "It is too late for that. The man I was is gone. The life I had is over. If the only thing I have to look forward to is being isolated while I predict bloody horrors and lose my sanity, I surrender and will gladly take my life's end."

"Oh, Shadow, no." Keyla grips my arm tight. "Don't say that. Promise me you won't hurt yourself. I mean it. Give us more credit. We'll figure this out. You have so much more life to look forward to."

"A few years, at most. The onset of madness in untrained oracles is swift and debilitating. The two of you admit you don't fully understand what is in store for me. I do. My life is over, whether I'm breathing or not."

Dillan stops walking. "You're not considering doing something stupid, are you, my man?"

As soon as possible. "Forgive me. I am simply distraught and speaking out of turn."

He curses. "And we're shifters and smell that lie. Fuck, Shadow, you gotta give us time to turn this around. I'm serious. There's no way we'll let you hurt yourself."

I finish my second beer, hand him the empty, and grab a third. "I wish to return to the hall now. I've had enough conversation for one afternoon."

CHAPTER THIRTEEN

Lukas

*W*hile Creed and Honor make their Amberloq announcements to the citizens of Dornte, Rhylan, Hawk, and I dive elbow-deep in goblin bullshit. The three of us are tracking how the economy works and where strengths and weaknesses lay in the production of the Dornte aror. Sadly, there are far more weaknesses than strengths.

"Oh, what a tangled web we weave," Hawk says staring at the breakdown of how the money flows in the quadrant. "Ruic Breard truly has his finger up everyone's ass, doesn't he?"

I chuckle at Rhylan's expression. "Yeah, our Barron has a poetic soul like that."

Hawk ignores me, picking up some of the bills lying on the war table to examine them again. "And you're certain that only the goblins know how to create this synthetic paper?"

Rhylan nods. "Yeah. The process is patented, and all of our press systems are tailored to those specifications."

"What do the other quadrants have?"

He shrugs. "They have different currency systems altogether.

Clarinta uses coins. Rames uses electronic credits. Travon uses paper and credits. And StoneHaven accepts all currencies of the four quadrants."

"How does that work when you're doing business between quadrants?"

"Fine, I guess, the banking systems convert to the currency of the receiving quadrant."

"Have you ever discussed having one currency as well as a quadrant currency?"

I smile. "Like the Euro?"

Hawk nods. "Similar to the Euro but with only four quadrants to balance, we could guard against some of the financial imbalances that tipped the scales in Europe."

"Shadow suggested something like that too. I think the idea has merit."

"What would happen to the aror citizens have in their banks and in their pockets?" Rhylan asks.

"Well, the aror would still work in the digital sense if Ruic tries to hold the quadrant hostage, but we'd have a secondary currency that is accepted as a Realm-wide dollar that could also be used. And, if the other quadrants want to adopt it going forward, there would be one currency going forward."

"But the dollar in Travon isn't worth the same amount as a dollar in Rames," Rhylan says.

"A value would have to be established for the transition period and that would be taken into account. So, if a citizen from Rames and Travon each had ten dollars in their accounts and Rames currency is considered twice as valuable as Travon, when you switch over to the unified currency the Rames citizen would be given twenty dollars for their ten and the Travon citizen would remain at ten."

Rhylan nods. "And who would be in charge of the production of this money? Dornte?"

Hawk shakes his head. "No. That wouldn't be fair. It would

have to be a joint venture between the four crowns and over-seen by StoneHaven. You told us many times that the architecture of your entire realm was preserved and restored there after the end of the Wars of Power, yes?"

"Yes."

"And StoneHaven used to be one realm with one currency, right?"

"Yes."

"So, we look into reviving an old mint or building a new one, and then establish an equal, four-way alliance with the other quadrants."

Rhylan doesn't look convinced. "What's in it for the other quadrants? Travon doesn't play well with others and I can guarantee you Rames won't join the union if there's not something over and above in it for them."

"I haven't got the incentives figured out entirely, but I've got some ideas—" Hawk stops talking and frowns as Creed and Honor join us.

Honor's expression tilts my world. "What? What's wrong? Did your citizen's address not go well?"

She shakes her head. "No. It went fine. Creed and I said our piece and answered the questions and I think the invitation to build our forces was received with a great deal of pride and excitement."

"So why do you look like you might throw up?"

She takes my hand and pulls me closer. "Because Doc just called Creed. He's putting Shadow on suicide watch. Apparently, he lied to them about not intending to hurt himself and locked himself in one of the bedrooms."

My stomach bottoms out and I lock my knees to keep from hitting the floor. Honor squeezes her grip and focuses on me. I tighten up before I make a scene. "Can you walk with me? I want to go straight back."

I take the opportunity as it's meant—as an opening to leave

without making excuses. "Of course. Hawk's got this. Excuse us."

I don't remember much about the trip back to Amberloq Hall except, once again, cursing the amount of time it takes to get from the castle to our Guardian headquarters and future home.

We gotta figure out something better for that.

My mind is a cyclone, my body filled with a level of chaos I haven't felt since my military days.

When we get inside, Doc meets us in the grand foyer. "Sorry to sound the alarm but he's not listening to us. Maybe you two can get through to him."

"Where is he?" I ask, my throat dry.

"The master suite."

My feet take me flying up the stairs, two at a time and I don't stop when I get to the end of the hall. I pass Keyla in the hall, send an opening spell forward, and hit the door with more magic than I intended to. The lock plate shatters as I bust through but I haven't got the energy to worry about that right now.

Shadow is sitting in the window seat, his knees up, his blind gaze locked toward the glass. "That didn't sound good."

"Not for the door, no," I say, my voice rough with the emotion. "It should've known better than to try to keep you from me when you're hurting."

"As crazy as it is... I'm sitting here, staring out this window as if that means anything. I feel the warmth of the sun on my face. I know there is a forest out there and the hedge maze and the city beyond. I picture it in my head and try to see it, but it fails to come."

I sit on the edge of the seat and reach over to wipe the tears from his cheeks. "You need to give yourself a damn minute to adjust. We haven't even begun to look into options. What you feel now isn't what you'll feel a month or even a year from now. You gotta give us time to fix this."

"There is nothing to fix. I am and have always been half-elf and half-oracle. As much as I prayed the latter would never come into play, it has. There is no turning it off. This is me now —a freak, an abomination, and soon, a mindless shell of a man."

I frown. "Don't say that."

"Why? It's the truth that is coming for me. Oracles without proper training and preparation go mad. I was tested as a child. If I had shown any signs then, I would have grown up within their cloistered community. I was deemed inactive and sent away."

"Then we talk to them now and get you help."

"It will make no difference. Their tenets are steeped in tradition. I won't be admitted, and honestly, I don't want to be. I would rather die out here amongst friends than live there as an outcast."

"Well, neither of those options work for me." I yank the laces of my boots, take them off, and swing around, bringing my knees up and mirroring his position. "You're not leaving. You're not going insane. And you're certainly not going to kill yourself."

"Those are not your declarations to make."

"Tough shit, I'm making them. You'll stay here. Doc and I will work on the oracle stuff, Honor and Creed can help with the mental stuff, and you'll live a long, happy life with people who love you."

His head falls back and I study the graceful line of his throat as he swallows. "That is a pretty picture you paint, soldier, but no one will ever look at me and say, Yeah, you know what? That's the man of my dreams. Let me sign on for a lifetime of torment and ridicule."

He lifts his head and stares at me as if he can see me despite being blind. "My life's purpose ended the moment I woke up from the accident."

The resignation in his words cleaves me in two.

He's giving up.

"You gotta stop spewing that poison."

"It's not poison, it is truth. My reality is—"

I move without thought, grip the front of his shirt and yank him toward me. Doing that to a blind man isn't the best idea. He stiffens, his hands flailing as he tries to regain his balance.

"Sorry. I didn't mean to manhandle you but you gotta stop talking about your reality as if you know what's in store. Your reality is that I love you."

The two of us freeze and I'm stunned those words flew out of my mouth as easily as they did.

I don't doubt them, I'm just surprised.

"No, you don't," he says. "You can't."

"I do, and I'm not letting you give up on yourself. If you can't believe in yourself, then believe in me. I won't let you do something so stupid as kill yourself. If you do, you'll be killing me too."

Shadow falls eerily still in my grip and it dawns on me that I should've gauged his interest in pursuing a relationship with me before blurting that out.

"Look, if you don't feel the same way, that changes nothing. Even as your friend, I won't let you—"

"Shut up," he whispers, his scowl deepening. "I don't want this."

My heart sinks. Yep. I definitely should have started with asking him his feelings first. "I'm sorry. I didn't mean to dump this on you. Even if it's one-sided, my point is—"

"Don't be stupid," he says, his eyes glassing up. "You can't love me."

"It's too late. I already do."

"No. You don't. Loving me will mean personal and political

suicide. I will be hated and feared. You need to get as far away from me as possible."

I fight the urge to shake him. "Shadow, I need you to hear me. I don't give two shits about stigmas or ridicule. I work for Hawk and he doesn't give two shits either. I'm committed to Honor... no shits given there either. There's no part of my life where someone's outside opinion will make me regret standing at your side."

"You say that now, but you don't understand."

"I guess I don't because I'm still hanging here with my heart on my sleeve. Is your only protest my well-being? I said I love you and you told me to shut up. Can you give me a hint about how you feel?"

He exhales, and another wave of those welling tears breaks loose. "No. It's not one-sided but we can't act on it... especially now."

"Why not?"

"For one, you're committed to Honor, the princess of this quadrant. You can't betray your love and I can't taint her standing."

"I talked to Honor. She's behind me—behind us."

The shock on his face is almost comical. "How? No, she can't be."

"I am."

I shift to find her and she's inside the bedroom and leaning against the door. Holding out my hand, I invite her to join us.

"Lukas is right. We talked and I understand where he is and what that means. You're part of this now unless you don't want to be."

"How could I not? It's not that—"

"No. It's *only* that," Honor says. "If you return Lukas's feelings and you want to be part of this crazy life we're living, then it's settled. Being a royal taught me many lessons over my lifetime but one of the most important was to not let the opinions or buzz of people outside my circle affect who I am or my decisions."

I nod and squeeze her hand. "Life is too short."

She winks and steps back. "I'm going downstairs to spend an hour or two in the chamber reviewing chronicle discs. I'll lock up downstairs, so we shouldn't be disturbed. Take a private moment. You've both been worn ragged and need some quiet time together."

I stand, pull her into my arms, and hug her tight against my chest. "I love you."

"And I love you. I told you. You are connected to my soul. Your heart is mine to protect."

"Same."

She eases back and presses her lips to mine. "I'd lock the door on my way out, but you destroyed it. Don't be surprised if I come back in an hour wet and wanton."

"You are always welcome." I look over to Shadow, wondering if I'm talking out of turn. "I guess Shadow and I should talk about things before I make promises."

Shadow shakes his head. "Elves are very open sexually and I have a deep respect and affection for you, Princess. If I am to be welcomed into your bed, you are evermore welcome in mine."

Fuck yeah, that idea lights me up in a hundred different ways.

Honor's grin is teasing as she pinches her bottom lip between her teeth. I wish Shadow could see it because it's making me harder by the second. "I better go or else I won't have the willpower to leave. An hour, two at the most, and then I'll be back."

I kiss her again. "Come back if you get bored."

"Make use of your time. I want you to have your first moments together privately. It's important."

"Gratitude, Princess."

Honor winks and then blows us a kiss as she leaves.

"She's an incredible female," Shadow says.

"She's one of a kind," I whisper, my emotions too close to the surface for my liking. "This will be amazing, Shadow. Trust me until I prove it to you."

"I look forward to you proving it."

The teasing in his tone snaps me out of my aching heart and brings me back to what this means.

I leave the window seat and pull him to his feet. Cupping his jaw in my palms, I lace my fingers behind his neck and pull him to my mouth. "After today, your mind and body will be branded with the pleasure of what I'm going to do to you. Every single cell in your body will know your life with me is more important than anything beyond your control. You are mine."

"Take from me that which is freely given."

CHAPTER FOURTEEN

Dune

No matter what scenario we come up with, there's no making sense of the destruction in this biome. It's not from the war with Laryssa... at least that we can tell. Bodies of the fallen have been left to decay instead of being returned to nature as is the fae tradition.

The buildings have all crumbled and fallen to ruin.

There's no sign of anyone in any of the villages we've searched and we've explored the entire biome.

"What the hell happened?" I turn to Tundra.

Even Tundra, the man who seems to know everything about everything, has no answers. "I don't know. Whatever it is, it was devastating."

"Is it an Elbirfae thing or a forested biome thing?"

Tundra's brow comes down hard. "I hadn't thought of that. When Laryssa and the Blood Witch killed off the Amberloq, do you think she killed off our biome communities as well?"

I shrug. "We went straight from Mount Nekko to Thornebane Castle. How do I know?"

"We must return to our home biomes immediately."

I scan the destruction of the jungle village and frown. "You don't think our families have suffered similar fates, do you?"

The look he flashes me twists my guts. "I don't know what to think. Go. Ensure all is well in the Desert Planes. Find out what you can. I'll meet you back at the castle as soon as I can."

I extend my palm and he clasps hold. "I wish your people well, T. May you find them happy and whole."

"You and yours as well. May the gods be with you."

"I'm sure they're fine. We'd sense it if they weren't. Wouldn't we?"

We push off the ground and up through the canopy of foliage into the open sky above. Pumping our wings, we gain momentum. I tilt to begin the long flight to the Desert Planes Biome and Tundra heads toward the Snowy Peaks.

Honor

It's nearly impossible to keep my mind on the history of Amberloq warriors and how things were originally set up, but I try. Lukas and Shadow need alone time to explore what's been building between them.

I close my eyes and groan.

I'm super turned on, knowing what's happening upstairs. If the entire quadrant wasn't depending on me to bring the Amberloq back from the ashes, I would run up there and join the welcome to our lives celebration.

Wow, Calli was right.

Being randy and wet is an inescapable by-product of having sexy men getting naked in rapid succession.

So much sexy time potential.

I hate that Shadow felt so lost he considered giving up. We'll work on that.

Calli was fortunate her mates were bound by fated bonds. There was no question that she was doing the right thing. With me, things are much more subjective.

Do I keep banging my head against the wall with Dune? Will Tundra resent us welcoming Shadow? How big is our bed going to have to be?

I laugh at that last one.

If we bind two king mattresses together, we'd have enough space to play. Four guys? Four strong, sexy, charismatic men. Oh, the fun we'll have...

Focus, dammit. I'm supposed to be working. How am I going to work when I'm this wound up?

I think about servicing myself and taking the edge off. I need to bring over BOB from my suite at the castle. I need more toys. I need some man toys. Ooo, two of them have feathers. Why haven't we incorporated those into play?

I roll my eyes, my panties damp with my lack of concentration.

Okay, seriously. I'm focusing. I check my watch and groan. "Thirty-two minutes down, twenty-eight minutes to go. I can do this."

I pull the disc on the hierarchy of power and set it to the side. Grabbing the next one, I slot it into the reader. This one is etched with crossed swords on it.

That likely means it's about weapons or battles.

That's not where my mind goes.

Dammit. This is the longest hour ever!

Shadow

When Lukas promised to brand my soul, he meant it. After a passionate round of strip me down and suck me off, he moved us out onto the private terrace off the Guardian's suite. I've had many lovers—elves often do—but in a field of many, he still stands out as exceptional.

It all happened so fast yet feels like I've been waiting for this my entire life. This is more than sex, he's claiming me. I want to remember every moment.

I only wish I could see him.

The warm breeze against my heated flesh feels amazing. Then there's the scent of his arousal mixing with the seduction oil he slicked over my skin. And then there's the sound of our bodies slapping as he takes me from behind.

In earnest.

I'm lost in the heat of him.

The hunger. The primal wanting. The penetration.

The erotic slide of our joining is deep, possessive, and thoroughly enjoyable. And he's not being gentle... which is more than all right by me.

My hands are clenched around the iron frame of a gazebo and I'm thankful the structure is bolted securely to the terrace floor. Lukas may not be a wildling or one of the other species with enhanced strength, but he is fighting fit and filled with passion.

For the first time in days, there is nothing but a mind-numbing pleasure and being consumed. There is nothing beyond the two of us bonding on the fourth-floor balcony of the Guardian's terrace.

He wraps my hair around his hand and closes his fist, tugging my head back. "You're a beautiful man, Shadow," he says behind me. "All sinew and corded muscle. No fat. No bulk. Just tanned skin, oiled and sweaty, glistening in the sun."

"If you'd let me, I'd admire your body as well."

His deep-throated chuckle sends a fiery pang to the base of

my sac. "Not yet. I plan on pleasuring you until you're sore. Every time you move for the next few days, you'll remember how much I want you, need you, and crave you. You'll never think of ending us, will you?"

My legs are shaking, from the onslaught, so I widen my stance. "No. It was a moment of desperation."

"That's the right answer." His fingers ease on my hips and he slows his rhythm. The switch from hard and hot to slow and sensual makes me realize how hard my heart is hammering in my chest.

I love everything about this.

"How are you doing?"

I think he's asking about my emotional state, but when he leans against my back and reaches around to grip my cock, I realize there's no response needed.

He'll see for himself.

My breath exhales in a rush as his slick hand strokes me from tip to root.

"You're doing well."

"Yes. Very."

"You're deliciously hard." I shudder as his grip tightens and his hand picks up speed. "I wish I could fuck you and suck on you at the same time."

"I would never last."

"Who are we kidding? Neither would I." His laughter rumbles against my back.

I close my eyes as his palming builds the pressure of my next release deep in my core. "I'll never last if you keep doing that either."

I'm not sure if I'm relieved or disappointed when he releases my cock. But then, he goes back to easing in and out of me and I forget to care.

Tundra

My journey to the Snowy Peak Biome is fraught with worry. Could my people have suffered the same fate as the forest Elbir-fae? Did the Blood Witch wipe out our species and not just our warriors?

It's too horrible to imagine, and yet, it's becoming a very real possibility.

And if it's a reality, what does that mean for rebuilding the Amberloq forces? It won't matter if King Creed lowered the application age if no one survived the raids to apply.

The thought of that makes me sick.

I left my community years ago and haven't been back but that doesn't mean I don't feel a deep connection to my people and my lands.

With strong flaps of my wings, I ride the heated thermals of summer until the air grows chilled and I see the white peaks of snow cresting the tops of mountain ranges.

I try to think back to the last time I was here.

Six years? Seven?

It was a couple of years after my acceptance into the Amber-loq. I was granted a four-day leave to return for the death of my mother and to oversee her return into the circle of nature.

Without her to anchor me to the community, I drifted away. I should've made a more committed effort to keep tabs on my community.

I failed them.

As the isolation of being the only one of my kind sets in, I search the skies ahead, scanning for the silhouettes of anyone out flying. I see none.

My heart presses at the base of my throat making it hard to swallow. This can't be happening.

Like Dune said. We would feel it if our entire race was extinguished.

Wouldn't we?

Dune

They're gone. I've combed the sandy seas from the Grinton Drift all the way over to the stony lands of Tanturn Terrace and found no encampments, no oasis settlements, no sign of my people.

How could this have happened?

Are the Elbirfae extinct?

It was hard enough on Tundra and me to think about being the only Elbirfae warriors to survive Laryssa's raids, but to be the only Elbirfae at all?

I can't even wrap my head around that.

Banking right, I soar toward the setting sun. When I left home almost five years ago, my tribe was settled in the crux of where the Craynin River surfaces in a cluster of three small oasis ponds.

It was a glorious place to grow up and I have nothing but the fondest memories of my life there. Maybe I can find out what happened to my family. Maybe there's some trace of something that will help me understand what happened. Because try as I might, none of this makes any sense to me.

My family can't be lost.

They just can't.

CHAPTER FIFTEEN

Lukas

"I bet Honor will be here soon." I run a lazy hand over the bare skin of Shadow's hip and stomach as I caress his body from behind. After thoroughly claiming him on the terrace, he said he needed to lay down or he'd fall down.

So, here we are.

"Honor loves sucking cock and will help us out."

"Are you certain... about Honor joining us?"

I swallow, my finger circling his nipple and toying with the pink tip. "Do you have reservations about her?"

"Only that she is precious and yours. The two of you don't need to make changes if—"

"—I'm sure. She was game from the moment I told her you were under my skin. And it's not just about me, if that's what you're thinking. She happens to see great things in you too."

I hear Honor on the stairs and chuckle, pulling the sheet over our hips. "Play like we're sleeping and she missed everything."

Shadow gathers my hand in his and snuggles in.

The two of us lay there playing sexed-out and I'm glad my face is turned into the pillow because I can't help but smile.

The heat of her gaze warms my flesh and I know she's in the room.

"Well... that's disappointing." Her whisper barely reaches us across the room.

I bark a laugh and give it up. "We're just screwing with you. We're not sleeping."

Honor's face is so relieved it's hilarious. "Good because I'm about to combust. I tried to be a good girl and study my homework but my heart and mind were up here being naughty."

Shadow chuckles. "Then come be naughty with us."

"Don't mind if I do."

As she shuffles closer, she pulls her top over her head and unbuttons her pants. Knowing that Shadow is missing the show, I decide to make sure he doesn't miss all the fun. "Leave the bra and panties on for us to remove, beautiful. Shadow deserves the tactile pleasure."

"Good point." She does as I ask and climbs onto the mattress at the bottom of the bed and crawls on all fours to join us. We separate to have her join us in the middle.

"How did the studying go? Anything life-altering?"

"Not yet, but my heart wasn't in it. I wanted to be up here welcoming Shadow to our love affair."

Shadow's smile is soft and a little sad. "That is kind of you."

Honor fusses with the sheet, kicking it down the bed so she's not separated from us. When she finishes, she's on her hip, facing him, and I have the glorious pleasure of spooning her ass. "It's not kindness, Shadow. It's fondness. You're an upstanding, intelligent, professional friend. You're also a very attractive guy."

"I second that."

She smiles over her shoulder at me and winks. "Lukas

knows you better than I and he fell hard for you. We both know he has wonderful taste in lovers, so that means, I welcome you to join us."

I run my hand over the round of her hip, the lace stretched to fit snuggly against her curves. "Give me your hand, Shadow."

He lifts his hand and I capture it, placing it over the lace I'm so taken with. "So that you can appreciate what I see, Honor is wearing a sexy dark blue underpants set. It's silky and shiny where it covers all her girl parts and then has this delicate lace that trims the edges. It's feminine and lovely."

Honor wriggles her ass against the cradle of my hips and smiles. "Consider me your private touch station, gentlemen."

Without the sheet to cover things, it's the work of a glance to see that Shadow is hard again.

I know exactly what our next round should be. The three-somes with Honor and the Elbirfae thus far have been on the wilder and raunchier side of things.

Our elf is a lover by nature. This should be tender.

"How about the two of us take our time stripping you down and then Shadow can make love to you while I watch and guide the fun?"

"That sounds lovely," Honor says.

Shadow dips his chin. "If there are no objections, I would be honored."

I get us started by gathering Honor's long, silver braid, and shifting it back between us and out of Shadow's way. "How about some get to know you kisses."

"Yes, please." Honor furthers the invitation by guiding his hand to her cheek and initiating the kiss.

The tenderness in the brush of their lips makes me ache. How can I love her more every moment? The two of them seem tentative at first, but after sexing Shadow up all afternoon, I think he's pretty relaxed.

And with Honor being her usual, sensual, loving self, the two of them are getting thoroughly familiar before long.

Leaning forward, I kiss the bare flesh of her shoulder. "I love you both. Thank you for making this work."

Honor slows the kiss and looks back at me. She's a little breathless and her cheeks are flushed. "It's no hardship. This boy can kiss."

"I know, right? And here you thought I just lost my mind the other night. Nope. He's addictive."

Shadow chuckles, nuzzling into the crook of her neck to continue his kiss. "I lost my sight. You know I can hear you, right?"

Honor grins and shifts to lay on her back. "It's not a secret. You *are* addictive."

I cup her jaw and run my thumb over her lips. When she bites my thumb, I decide to get this show on the road. "Go ahead and take off her underpants, Shadow. Any way you want. Slow and teasing. Quick and rough. You do you."

Our elf smiles, shifts down the mattress, and feels her hips until he's where he wants to be. Then, he leans forward and presses his mouth to her navel. With a teasing tongue, he rims her belly button, caressing the tender flesh.

The sound Honor makes as she arches against the mattress is all feminine pleasure. Her knees fall open and she reaches down, burying her fingers into the striking purple of his hair.

My body responds and my cock hardens.

Shadow moves lower, pressing his kisses to the silk, and blowing a hot breath through the fabric to her core.

Honor's nipples tighten beneath the silk of her bra and I reach over to give those tightened buds a gentle tweak. "Fuck, you're beautiful."

As I take in the sights, Shadow hooks the lace against her hips and tugs her panties down her long legs. Once her feet are free, he passes the wad of blue silk up to me and smiles. "Without being able to see where I'm going down here, I need to feel my way around."

Honor chuckles. "Whatever you need, sweetie."

He lowers his face to the smooth flesh of her thigh and begins a slow exploration. Honor's eyes roll closed and her body melts against the mattress. "That feels wonderful."

"Your skin is incredibly soft," he says, brushing his cheek against the inside of her leg. "Open wider for me, *lirimaer*."

I shift back a bit, slide my hand behind her knee, and gently hold her open as he nuzzles at the opening of her core. "Your arousal is heady. Thank you for letting me consume your essence."

"You're welc—oh, yes. Consume away."

~

Honor

I swallow, my head kicking back as Shadow takes me by mouth. He says my arousal is a heady scent but he and Lukas have been messing around up here for over an hour and their skin is a glorious manly mixture of sweaty male, sex, and hunger.

"You really are wound up, aren't you, Princess?" Lukas's voice is sexy as sin itself. It gets this deep rasp to it when he's really turned on and with his accent, it's beyond erotic.

It's like that now.

His hold on my knee is keeping me pinned open for Shadow. And yeah, that's doing it for me.

"Stroke his ears," Lukas says. "An elven erogenous zone is the peaked tips of their ears. You love that, don't you, Shadow?"

He nods, flicking his tongue against the tightened nerves of my clit as he works against my entrance.

I'm so lost in the bliss of being devoured, it takes time for Lukas's words of encouragement to sink in.

Right, his ears.

I release my fingers from the depths of his hair and focus on caressing the peaks of his ears.

His response is immediate.

He groans against my heated flesh and dives in. Sliding his hands beneath my butt, he lifts my hips pulling me into his mouth. With the intensity of the attention, the knowledge that I'm driving him wild, and how horny I've been for the past hour downstairs, there's no holding back my climax.

I close my eyes as the keening of sensation builds and the pulse and constrict starts to take hold.

"That's it, beautiful," Lukas whispers, nipping my neck. "Come against his mouth, Princess. Let him lap at your cream and sate his thirst. Then, he's going to shift up your body and fill you, aren't you, Shadow?"

"Mhmm," he mumbles against my core.

I groan. The vibration of his answer tickles me in all the best ways.

"She's close, Shadow. Make her cream hard. Don't be afraid to play with your fingers. Honor likes to be finger fucked, don't you?"

"Yes."

"Knees up, Princess," Lukas says. "Don't be shy. Let him have full access to all your goodies."

I'm blatantly spread open now and I swallow, my mouth flooding with saliva because yes, I'm salivating for everything these two are promising me.

The moisture they call from me makes everything wet and Shadow plays front to back, slicking me up.

I'm almost panting, expecting Shadow to finger me and continue with his mouth...

It catches me off guard when his thumb plunges inside me,

his fingers brush over my clit, and he moves his mouth to my ass.

I arc, not sure I like it at first. It's a very strange sensation to have a man's tongue probing there.

It seems dirty and taboo...

Is it an elf thing? It's a first for me but yeah, I think I do like it. Should I like it? Why do I like it? Why am I questioning it?

There's something super powerful about toying with the taboo. It makes me even more wanton and horny than I was. And then there are his fingers on my clit, his thumb delving inside me, oh, and that dirty mouth of his...

My orgasm hits hard and I shatter. Lost to the pleasure of what's being done to me, my body convulses in racking spasms. Lukas has a hold of both my knees now, holding me open for Shadow.

I should be embarrassed. Shouldn't I?

And still that tongue of his probes my anus. I've always liked ass play and small toys. I didn't expect this.

"Take her, Shadow. Ride out her orgasm and let's see where this takes us."

Where this takes us?

Shadow releases his possession of all things dark and dirty and crawls up my body. His blind eyes are glowing like they did when he was possessed with a premonition but I think he's possessed with something else at the moment.

I run my hands up his ribs and guide him up my body. Reaching between us, I urge him to my entrance and then use my heels on his ass cheeks to pull him in.

"Oh, she's hungry," Lukas says, chuckling. "Watch her when she gets like this. She's rough and she bites."

Shadow chuckles but doesn't seem daunted in any way. He pushes inside me and we both groan at the glorious fit. Shadow's cock is hard and thick and hits me in all the right places.

I open my legs again and figure, why bother being modest now. "Lukas, make yourself useful and hold my legs again."

He chuckles, stands on the bed, and straddles us, taking hold of my ankles. "Nice view from up here."

It's a nice view for me too.

I've got Shadow rocking inside me and Lukas naked and standing over us, his cock probing out from his body like the javelin of a proud knight.

Is this my new life?

If so—me likey.

"How are you doing, Shadow?" Lukas asks. His voice is that deep rasp again and it makes me pulse even more. "Being inside her is fucking heaven, isn't it?"

"It is. Do you mind if I monopolize her for say... the next month or so?"

"Sounds good to me."

If only.

I've never been the kind of girl who gets lost in the pleasures of men—not in the Fae Realm before the raids and not in the Human Realm as Riley—but this is a next-level pleasure. And knowing it's not fleeting or temporary makes things that much more intense.

The delicious friction of flesh as Shadow fills me and then recedes to fill me again is mesmerizing—intoxicating. It's sexy to the extreme, especially with his mouth on my collarbone and his hair dangling forward and brushing over my breasts.

"How sore is your ass from our playtime earlier, Shadow?"

Shadow chuckles, his body vibrating against mine. "I have no complaints."

I meet Lukas's gaze over Shadow's shoulder and arch a brow. "Are you thinking about tagging into this game, magic man?"

He grins, stroking himself. "I don't want to take away from your fun, but I thought taking him while he's taking you might be a viable option."

I laugh. "Always the tactician, aren't you?"

His grin is too sexy. "Or I can play the sideline and take care of myself. That works too."

Shadow shakes his head. "No. If you desire me, I am ready and willing to please you. To have both of you at once sounds wonderful."

"Widen your knees around her," Lukas says, dropping to his knees behind Shadow. I hear the pop of a plastic lid and smile.

That's Lukas. Always prepared for any eventuality.

I know the moment he's slicking Shadow up because the elf's breath escapes and the rhythm of his thrusts falters.

And then he stills.

"I'll play a bit and make sure you're ready for me," Lukas says. "I know I said I want you sore for days, but I want that to be from being well used, not from negligence on my part."

Shadow's eyes are closed as his hips stop thrusting. "There is nothing negligent about you as a lover. You are very thorough."

He grins as his gaze drops to focus. In my mind's eye, I see him lining his swollen crown up. I know from being Lukas's lover that he'll make sure everything is moist and will slide. He'll make sure Shadow is wet and relaxed and ready to accept him.

And then he'll push inside.

Shadow gasps and braces his palms. I trace a thumb across the sweat dampening his brow and revel in the fullness of my insides. Having Lukas inside him has made Shadow even thicker than before.

And then Lukas starts to rock his hips. "Everybody good?"

"So good," I say, enjoying the chain reaction of Lukas pumping into Shadow while Shadow is inside of me. "I think this is the perfect way for the two of us to welcome Shadow. Both of us at once."

"Couldn't agree more," Lukas says. "I know there is an entire realm of things waiting for us to get done, but they have to wait.

We need this. I need to fuck the two of you and start this off right."

Lukas falls quiet then, the only sound to follow is the slap of flesh and the breathy grunt of my two lovers.

"Harder," I groan, gripping Shadow's shoulders. "I want you to drive Shadow into me."

"Palms against the headboard, Princess," Lukas says. "Brace yourself."

I reach behind my head and lock my arms as Shadow adjusts his palms as well. "You good, Shadow?"

"Perfect. Yes. Fuck me like you love me."

"Yes, sir."

The world melts away from us after that. Three connected bodies lost in the enthrallment of pounding strokes and sweat and primal pleasure.

And then, I open a mental link.

From one thrust to another I'm not only feeling my pleasure but Lukas's and Shadow's as well.

The sense of peace Shadow feels being buried inside me as my inner muscles constrict around his cock is incredible. Each time Lukas hits home his pleasure ratchets higher and we claim a little more of his heart.

And then there's Lukas. The depth of his aching want for both of us is immeasurable. His possession, his need to protect us, his need to pleasure us—his love.

There's no question about it.

I reach across the mental plane and allow them full access to my sensations, the building of my next orgasm, and how their pleasure and primal need drives me closer to release.

"Not yet, Shadow," Lukas says.

Shadow laughs. "Not yet yourself. It's too good."

Agreed.

I take pity on Shadow and call my release forward. I'm close enough that the mere thought starts the throbbing pulse of the first wave.

Shadow stiffens and connected as we are, I feel his release bear down on him. He stiffens as his hips lock and Lukas curses behind him.

The clench of Shadow's ass as he stiffens grips Lukas hard and sets him off too.

It's a domino effect of orgasm and it's magical.

The three of us are lost to our own releases for a time, our bodies consumed by satisfaction. As we come down from the high of orgasm, we pant and catch our breath until each of us is spent and then we fall to the mattress in a heap of sated sweat.

"That was awesome," I breathe, sandwiched between the two of them.

"It was," Shadow says, "but if I suffer a coronary, I want Lukas held responsible."

Lukas chuckles behind me and brings the sheet up to cover us before a chill sets in. "I'll take the heat for that. It'll be worth it."

"Oh, it was worth it, but I'll still be dead."

I reach forward and kiss his shoulder. "I'm glad he didn't sex you to death, Shadow. It would've ruined some of the most fun I've ever had naked."

He brushes a hand against my cheek and then covers his mouth as he yawns. "I am exhausted. Any chance we can take a cat nap?"

"I vote yes. The world will have to wait a little longer. We'll work hard when we wake up, won't we, magic man?"

Lukas doesn't answer so I twist to look behind me. "He's already out cold."

Shadow chuckles quietly, jiggling the bed. "Then I guess we should close our eyes."

I reach forward again and snuggle into him. "Thank you, by the way. That was amazing and truly special."

"It was. Though, if Lukas has his way, I won't be able to sit or walk straight for a week."

"You do have an exceptionally nice ass."

"Thanks. Yours is incredible too."

I think about the sexplay and my cheeks heat and flush. I have a feeling adding an elven lover to the mix is going to be very interesting.

I'm looking forward to every minute.

CHAPTER SIXTEEN

Honor

The three of us must've really burned each other out because we didn't wake up from our nap until ten hours later. Either life had been demanding too much from us or we were just that sated and comfortable snuggled in our bed… whatever the reason, we didn't rouse until Lukas jumped up and grabbed his gun from the bedside table.

"Be at ease," Tundra says, holding up his hand. "I didn't mean to disturb you, but there are things that must be discussed."

You know when you're so deep in sleep you don't have a clue if it's day or night? Yeah, that's where I am. I check my watch and stretch, checking the window to ensure it's six a.m. and not six p.m.

I look him over and it's easy to see he hasn't gotten much sleep since the last time we saw him. He has had a shower though. His ebony hair is still damp and curling by his ears. "Are you all right, Tundra?"

"No. Not even a little."

"Should I go?" Shadow asks.

I reach over. "No. You're perfect where you are. You're part of this now. We are five."

Tundra follows my meaning. "Five."

Lukas nods. "Sorry, my friend. There was no fighting it. Shadow is ours and has been from the beginning."

He takes a minute and then nods. "Welcome to the chaos. I look forward to getting to know you better."

As funny as that seems to me as a welcome to our sexual quadrangle, I let it go. There's time to get everyone on the same page later.

"What do you need to talk to us about?" Lukas asks, grabbing his pants off the floor and searching for his shirt over by the window.

"How about I put on the kettle and heat something for breakfast and you three pull yourself together?"

"As Calli would say, thank you baby Groot." I laugh at the bewilderment in his face. "Hanging out in the human realm taught me all kinds of nonsensical things. Just nod."

"Yes, Princess."

I'm up and jogging toward the ensuite when I turn back to meet his gaze. "And stop calling me Princess, like that. We're lovers. Think of a pet name or something. The way you say princess makes me feel like I'm sexing my employees."

Lukas follows me into the bathroom, dumps his clothes on the counter, and goes straight for the shower. I rush into the toilet cubicle to empty my bladder. When I'm finished in there, I wash up, and then grab my brush off the counter.

I haven't brought much over from the castle but I did bring a toiletry bag and a few pieces of clothing. It'll be enough to pull myself together as Tundra put it.

Pulling the brush through my hair, I get the tangles taken care of and then braid it to keep it out of the way in the shower. By the time I get to the shower, Lukas is stepping out and we change places.

"I warmed it up for you." He grabs a towel off the warming rack and steps onto the bathmat to dry off.

"That was very kind of you." I make quick work of sudsing and rinsing and avoid getting my hair wet.

By the time I'm stepping out, Lukas is escorting Shadow in to take the next shift. "Looking good, elf man," I say, running my hand across his abs. "Too bad we're in a rush, I would join you in the shower and play dutiful mansion wife with you."

Shadow chuckles. "Is that a thing?"

Lukas laughs. "It is now. I say we implement that as soon as possible."

"Agreed."

I accept the towel from Lukas and grin. "Look at the three of us all domestic and everything. This is a great way to start our day."

"Although it isn't starting off to be a great day, by the sounds of it." Lukas squeezes a glob of toothpaste onto a brush. "Tundra looked both worried and exhausted."

"He did. Well, after he tells us what's wrong, he can have a nap and we'll take over."

Shadow chuckles. "Is anyone else a little disoriented that our post-coitus nap lasted all evening and through the night?"

Lukas spits into the sink, rinses, and spits again. "It was a long and stressful day."

"But it did have a few major high points," I add.

"Definitely true." Lukas strides over to the shower once Shadow turns off the water. "Here, let me help you." He takes a dry towel off the rack and gets Shadow clear of the shower and wrapped in heated terry.

"Thank you for the help. I hate to be more of a bother, but could one of you grab my clothes?"

"Of course, sweetie. I have to find mine too." I shuffle back to the bedroom to begin the search.

My shirt and pants are easy enough to find. I stripped them

off in the middle of the floor while walking toward the bed. Shadow took off my underwear over... there.

I see a flash of navy silk under the flap of one of the pillows and collect it. Lukas took off my bra. Where did he toss... bingo.

With my clothes sorted, I find Shadow's with little effort. His stuff is all piled in the chair by the window seat where we found him yesterday.

Wow, was that only yesterday?

I take all the clothing back with me into the bathroom. Sadly, Lukas is already dressed, so I missed the show. I do get the pleasure of watching Shadow dress while I put on my clothes.

I rush to the sink to brush my teeth once all my body parts are covered. Straightening, I give myself a quick look in the mirror. "This is as good as it gets in a rush."

Lukas chuckles. "You could be wearing a paper bag and be blow-the-load gorgeous."

I do a quick minty scrub and then bend to spit. "That's my silver-tongued charmer. Blow-the-load gorgeous. That's classy."

"Thank you."

When I turn to leave, I realize Shadow's shirt is on inside out. I'm about to let him know when Lukas shakes his head. "Everybody all set?"

I nod. "Yep. Let's go let Tundra ruin our day."

Tundra

I wait for the others in the kitchen, my heart heavy. Part of me thinks if I say it out loud there is no going back. There is no going back either way. There's also no use in denying it. The Elbirfae are gone.

At some point, some time ago, my species was extinguished.

I pour myself a coffee, take a sip, and realize it's not strong enough. A quick trip to the bar in the common area brings me back with a bottle of whiskey to top off.

"That bad is it?" Lukas comes in with Honor and Shadow, the three of them fresh from the shower and looking apprehensive.

"I'm afraid so. Dune and I searched the jungled forests. In every town and every settlement, it was the same thing. Nothing remains except destruction and death long forgotten. It got us both thinking about our communities, so we split up and returned to our biomes. I can't say for certain what Dune found, because he isn't back, but I suspect it will be no different than what awaited me in snowy peaks."

"And what was that?" Honor steps away from the others and stands before me. Her purple gaze is warm and sympathetic. Normally I would appreciate the shared emotion but at the moment I'm trying to hold it together in front of my peers.

I shift my gaze to Lukas and harden up. "I found the remains of my people, the destruction of buildings, and no sign of survivors."

Lukas's demeanor grows more severe. "What are you thinking, Tundra? If you had to guess, what happened?"

"The bodies we found were long dead. I'm no forensic expert but I think the attack coincided with Laryssa's raids and the slaughter of the Amberloq. We thought she and the Blood Witch simply targeted the warriors, I now believe she targeted my whole species."

"Genocide of an entire fae species?" The horror in Honor's words is like a dagger to my soul.

"I'm afraid so, Princess. I'd like to spend more time searching and possibly tracking down the few who may have escaped but understand that our priority must be the dangers of today and not the actions of the past."

Lukas nods. "You're right about that, Tundra, but I'll speak to Hawk and see if we can import a few FCO teams to dispatch to start the investigation."

"We might do well to bring on some enforcers as security for the Crown for the short-term too," Shadow suggests. "If Vikarus and Ruic are aware of the massacre they will be emboldened to strike before the Amberloq numbers have a chance to be rebuilt."

"Agreed." Lukas pulls out his cell and starts typing a message. "And considering Vik just ended up on our doorstep snooping around, I bet they'll strike soon."

"Something to look forward to then," Honor says, opening the fridge to pull out the ingredients needed to make breakfast. "I guess my public invitation to invite Amberloq applicants is making Ruic and his followers feel pretty smug right about now."

"Fuck them," Lukas says finishing his text. "Our plans haven't changed. We just need to compensate and realize we've now become the undisputed underdogs."

Honor sets a crate of eggs as well as a handful of peppers and mushrooms onto the counter. "Well everyone loves to root for the underdogs, right?"

"Right you are, Princess." Shadow leans up against the marble island. "And the payout is always better because they won against the odds."

Lukas chuckles. "What exactly is the payout here, elf? Are we getting paid?"

Honor chuckles and looks at the three of us. "Fighting for justice is its own reward."

Lukas takes out two wooden cutting boards and pulls the knife block closer to start chopping. "Says the wealthy Princess of the realm."

She laughs and pulls out a couple of large mixing bowls. "You boys will be paid well in sexual favors."

Lukas chuckles and checks in with me and Shadow. When

he looks back at her, he breaks into a lascivious smile. "We accept your terms."

Lukas

After breakfast, Honor and I spend half an hour working on her strength training and hand-to-hand combat. She's getting stronger and quicker every day. She spends the next hour in her library listening to the discs while Tundra and Shadow clean up, and I coordinate with Hawk to bring a sizable force of warriors through the portal gate.

"The Quint will be here within the hour," I say, finishing with a text conversation with Hawk over at the castle. "Hawk's at the portal hub now awaiting the arrival of Kotah, Calli, and Jaxx."

"It's a shame they need to keep coming back and forth," Shadow says. "Kotah has enough to worry about in the other realm with the reign of the fae there."

"They've moved to the Pennsylvania property, so it's not so far. Their new home and compound are breaking ground and they want to be there to oversee the construction. For them to come here is as easy as walking through the gate and catching a shuttle. It's not so bad. Besides, we need to talk to them about Shadow's prophecy and how it might relate to their baby."

Shadow frowns. "I am sorry to be the source of concern for your friends."

"Not your fault." I slip my phone back into my pocket and close the distance between me and my elf. "Nothing about you being an Oracle was your choice. No matter how this plays out it's not your fault. You are merely a messenger. No one will judge you for it."

"I think you're being overly optimistic."

I chuckle. "I can honestly say, no one has ever accused me of being overly optimistic. I am solidly grounded in reality. You'll see."

Shadow doesn't look convinced but there's nothing I can say in this moment that will change his mind. Only time can do that. I lean in and give his lips the gentle brush with mine. "Keep the faith. You promised you would trust in me until you start to believe it yourself."

Shadow nods. "I did and I will."

"Listen, I have a few more things to finish up here before Hawk and the others arrive. Would you like to sit on the patio for a while? The sun is out and by the swaying of the trees it looks like there is a breeze."

"That would be nice. Thank you."

After I get Shadow settled on the outdoor sofa off the kitchen, I take the opportunity to make things right with Tundra.

He's sitting alone at the kitchen table sipping his spiked coffee. The guy looks wrecked. It's understandable. Everyone he grew up with and loved has been killed. "I am so incredibly sorry for your loss, my man. I can't even imagine what you're going through. If I can help in any way, just ask."

He looks at me over the rim of his mug and nods. "I appreciate that, thank you."

I slide into the chair opposite him and fold my hands on the table. "I also need to apologize to you."

"Whatever for?"

"You came home from one of the most horrific moments in your life and found Honor and I in bed with Shadow. That shouldn't have happened. I'm sorry."

"We're all adults navigating a very new situation. I don't have the right to judge or the energy to be upset."

"That's not true. You have every right to be upset. When you and Dune left, the dynamic between the four of us was cast even if it was a little tenuous. Honor and I altered the agreement. We welcomed Shadow into our lives and you didn't get a chance to weigh in."

"So, it's a bonding and not just a liaison?"

"It is."

"And you love him?"

"I do and I don't regret that, but it would sit better with me if we spoke to you and Dune before we acted on anything."

"In the end, whether we knew before or after, the result is the same. You love him. He is a part of us. We will make it work." When his gaze locks with mine there's no doubt in his expression.

"That's very gracious of you."

"You've been very gracious with us."

I've tried. "If you and Dune don't feel the same way about Shadow as Honor and I do, I want you to know that's all right. The five of us don't have to be one hundred percent with each other. We can make room for all different kinds of relationships."

Tundra sets his mug onto the table and gives me his full attention. Reaching forward, he places his hand over mine. The lean-in causes his wings to adjust and damn, those feathers are breathtaking. "I can't speak for Dune, but I have no problem with Shadow joining us in a romantic relationship. And considering Dune was raised in a communal family, I can't imagine he will either."

The two of us think about that for a moment and break into laughter.

"All right, initially Dune will have a big problem with it, but it won't last. He's more than the man he shows to the world. Give him time. I still believe he will rise to his calling."

I'm not so sure, but then again, I don't know Dune like he does. I clasp hands with the snow warrior across the table. "You are a good man, Tundra. I'm proud to be in a quint with you."

The two of us share a moment and then ease back in our seats. Although I respect Tundra, and we've had a few shared moments with Honor, the love and desire I feel for Shadow and Honor aren't fully formed with Tundra yet.

I'm hopeful we'll get there but for now, mutual affection, attraction, and respect are good enough.

"Should we expect Dune's return anytime soon?"

Tundra lifts one of his mighty shoulders in a shrug. "From where I left him in the forested biome, the desert planes was farther to travel but I expect he will return shortly."

"So, we should enjoy the peace while it lasts?"

"Exactly."

The two of us are still chuckling about that when the front door buzzer sounds. I pull my tablet out of the thigh pocket of my fatigues and call up the video feed for the front porch. "It's the quint. I'll let them in. Could you gather Shadow and Honor and meet us in the common room? I'm hoping they brought a surprise I requested and I'd like a quick second to ask in private."

Tundra nods. "Of course. We'll be right there."

I leave Tundra and make my way through the massive mansion of Amberloq Hall. By the time I reach the grand entrance, the excitement is getting to me.

From the view of the camera, I couldn't see if they brought what I asked for... but I have a good feeling.

Ha! Since when am I optimistic?

Maybe Shadow's right and being in love really has turned my frown upside down.

The *clack* of metal bolts signals the release of the locks and after I remove my warding on the front door, I swing open the heavy panel. "Welcome back. Come in and join the fun."

The five of them look like they're all about to break into hysterics. Jaxx and Calli take the lead, the two of them all smiles and snickers.

Knowing them as I do, I'd guess the Texan cowboy probably just said something incredibly inappropriate and they're all trying to hold it together.

"Do I want to know?" I direct the question at Hawk.

"Definitely not."

"Good enough for me." As Brant steps inside and I can see around him, my excitement bolsters. "Oh, he's perfect."

Kotah smiles, stroking a protective hand over the furry ruff of an ebony and silver wolf cub. "Perfect, yes, but he is a *she*."

"Hello, sweet girl." I hold my hand out and give her a chance to sniff my scent. "May I?"

"Of course," Kotah says, handing me the pup.

I cradle the young wolf against my chest, stroking her ebony cheek, while she licks my fingers.

"Who do you have there, magic man?"

I meet Honor's gaze and smile. "She's a spirit wolf. I asked Kotah to pull a few strings for me and see if he could arrange for her to be brought here for Shadow."

"For me?" Shadow says, looking confused. "A pet wolf to keep me company?"

"No, not at all. Most people are aware that witches and mages can bond with a familiar. It's a way for us to extend the reach of our power into another being. In rare cases, if the magic wielder knows what they're doing, that bond can be established in the reverse direction as well."

I see by the look on his face, he's not following.

"Spirit wolves are known protectors in many of the native fae sects. They grow larger than ordinary wolves and often take a rider. The bond that builds between animal and companion is profound."

"A rider?" Shadow repeats. "I've heard tales of elven wolf riders."

"Exactly. Spirit wolves are best matched with elves because of their shared connection with nature. It's a great honor to be entrusted with a cub, and if you'll hold her, I'll show you why she's here."

I stride over to Shadow and, between Honor and I, we get the cub settled and secured in the cradle of his arms. "Now, comfort her and focus on connecting with her. I'll do the rest."

It's a testament to Shadow's trust in me that he doesn't ask more questions. It also means it will be a better surprise when I'm done.

Focusing on the two of them, I place one hand over Shadow's blank eyes and my other over the eyes of the wolf. "The younger the animal the easier the imprinting is and the stronger the link between the two. She's perfect... exactly the cub I was hoping for."

I close my eyes and call forward a massive store of magical energy. My spell isn't complex. It takes a great deal of power and is rare, but rarer because usually those capable of performing it would never allow the transfer of power to go to the animal as well as from it.

That's not the case here.

In a matter of moments, I've opened the connection between wolf and man, their fates locked and intertwined as companions from this day forward.

When I pull my hand back, the hair on my arms stands on end. The magic of the wolf is strong in the air.

"Open your eyes, Shadow."

He does as I ask and falls eerily still. "What happened. How?" He looks around and the confusion morphs into a panic. "What's wrong? Why can I see you but not the room when I turn my head?"

I circle to stand behind him wrapping my arms around to turn him and the wolf cub toward our friends. "You're seeing out of her eyes. Oracles are blind. There's nothing I can do to change that. When the universe gave you prophetic sight it took your eyesight, but, with a spirit wolf companion, you'll never be truly blind and isolated from your surroundings."

"That's fucking cool," Hawk says.

I turn Shadow to face me and look straight into the wolf's one gold and one blue eye. "You will never be lost in the dark as long as I am here to light you a path. I swear it."

CHAPTER SEVENTEEN

Shadow

She is incredible. Despite my wolf companion making me slightly nauseous as she bounds around the room, I couldn't feel more blessed. She may be a spirit wolf by nature but to me, she is more than that. She is freedom and reclaimed independence.

She is a life restored.

Honor sits beside me on the couch and even though I'm looking at her, I'm seeing the back of the curtains across the room.

This displaced vision is disorienting.

Still, I'll never complain. Even after mere days of being stuck in a sightless world, being gifted with this fragmented sight and, in the future, normal sight, my entire outlook has changed.

"What will you name her?"

"I think Moonshade. Lukas said her fur is as dark as the night sky and she has a beautiful champagne crescent around her neck like a quarter moon. Is that right?"

"It is. She's beautiful. I think Moonshade is a perfect name for her. Do you really see what she sees?"

I nod. "It's odd to be facing you and watching her paws bat at the back of the couch. Lukas said that as she grows, she'll learn about our bond and will know to be my eyes when I need her. Until then, I might get a little seasick."

Honor laughs. "She'll never get away with doing something bad. You'll always know it was her because you'll see it."

"That's true. Although, I can't see myself ever faulting her for anything. She's a truly wonderful gift. I will love her and rise to the honor of being her elf companion. I swear it."

Honor squeezes my hand and leans in to kiss my cheek. "There's no doubt in my mind."

The two of us spend the next ten minutes chatting and chasing my wolf out from behind cupboards and curtains in the community room before Keyla arrives with Creed and Doc.

"Let me hug the newest member of our family," Keyla says.

I point across the room. "Moonshade is under the table by the door. She's currently obsessed with the power cable for the lamp."

Keyla chuckles. "I didn't mean your wolf cub, silly. I meant you. Creed just told me the exciting news. You're now with Lukas and Honor? Congrats."

"Oh, thank you. Yes, it is very new but we're excited. If the last twenty-four hours are any indication, I think we're well-matched and off to a great start."

"A fantastic start," Honor adds.

I stand to accept the hug of welcome to the Thornebane family. It all seems so surreal. I am a lifemate to the princess of the realm and a male like Lukas. Mayhap, in time, I might even bond with Tundra and Dune.

"You deserve every happiness, my friend," Keyla says, squeezing me and kissing my cheek.

Moonshade catches the scent of the new arrivals and comes

barreling towards the couch at full speed. Her paws are massively too big for her body, and it makes her clumsy. When her footing changes from hardwood to the area rug, she topples in a furry ball, landing at Keyla's feet.

"Oh my. Aren't you the most beautiful little thing? How precious. Hello sweet girl."

Moonshade looks up as Keyla scoops her off the floor and snuggles her in. "Mmm, she smells like evergreens and summer breezes."

"Exactly what I thought."

The two of them settle on the couch opposite us and I reclaim my seat next to Honor.

Keyla's laughter is infectious as Moonshade laps and licks her face with a million kisses. "I love that there's another wolf in the family. In my opinion, there can never be too many."

Creed chuckles, sitting beside her to get in on the love. "If you ever feel like filling our lives with cubs, your husbands won't object."

Keyla rolls her dark brown eyes and goes back to kissing Moonshade. "I haven't even had my twentieth birthday. I'm not ready to rear cubs and be bound as a mother. I'm still enjoying being the focus of three hot and horny men."

Honor laughs. "It's a full-time distraction, isn't it?"

"It takes getting used to." Keyla buries her face in the fur of my little black wolf and giggles. "There is a definite period of adjustment. No complaints though."

Honor shakes her head. "Oh, I wasn't complaining."

"Wasn't complaining about what?" Calli asks, striding in with Brant to join us.

Honor stands to hug her best friend. "Keyla and I were discussing the balancing act of having multiple hot and horny men as husbands."

"And absolutely not complaining," Keyla adds.

"Well good," Brant says, puffing up his chest. "We men work hard so you women have nothing to complain about."

"Work, work, work," Jaxx says joining us. "It's a full-time job to keep a powerful female sated."

Calli barks a laugh. "You can't possibly be blaming this on me. Do you remember how I got pregnant? That was all you guys."

Brant lets off a deep rumbling chuckle as Jaxx's face breaks into a sexy grin. "Darlin', I remember everything about that afternoon. If it hadn't already been called the Stud Suite, it would be now."

Keyla slaps her hands over her ears. "Lalalala, please stop. I think for the sanity of siblings we need to keep some of our sexual exploits private. No one wants images in their head of their brother or sister getting naked and raunchy."

"Very true," Creed says, making a face at Honor.

Calli plunks down on one of the other couches and runs a hand over the rounded mound of her belly. "All joking aside, Lukas told us Shadow had a premonition that may or may not involve our baby. Can we get into that? I'd like to know what we're dealing with."

Honor looks around the room until she finds Tundra. "Can you show them the video, please?"

"Yes, Princess."

She chuckles. "And could one of you boys assist Tundra and Shadow with a term of endearment for me that doesn't make me feel like they might break into a bow? I've asked them a hundred times to not be so formal with me. Obviously, they need help to unwind."

"Challenge accepted," Brant says. "I got you. I am the king of unwinding, seconded only by the Jaguar."

Jaxx grins. "I appreciate the mention."

Honor

Tundra pulls up the video and hands Calli the phone. She, Jaxx, and Brant huddle in close to watch the screen. Having seen it a couple of times I know how alarming Shadow is during an oracle moment.

I don't blame them for their steely looks. Glancing over to Keyla and Creed, I'm thankful to see the sweet little wolf cub has fallen fast asleep in Keyla's lap.

That means, Shadow doesn't have to witness his friends reacting to his new reality.

The child of fire, the moon of light,
A sea of blood to stain the night,
The foe of freedom, the king is down,
A war of outcasts to hold the crown.

When the video is over Jaxx lets off a long sigh. "It doesn't paint a full picture of what we're looking at but I agree, our little spark plug could be the child of fire."

Kotah joins us, his expression drawn in a somber frown. Knowing the heightened hearing of wildling wolves I have no doubt he heard everything from the other room. "The thing to keep in mind about an oracle premonition is that it's a glimpse into what *might* happen. It's not a bound destiny like so much in our world. More often, it's a warning to prepare you for what's coming."

"But if what's comin' is the part about the foe of freedom taking the king down, we need to figure out a plan to keep that from happenin'."

"Jaxx is right," Hawk says, coming in with Lukas. "We've sent for military force, but it'll take time to not only mobilize them but get them through the gate and get them here."

"What's the ETA?" Brant asks.

"The first wave will arrive in the next four or five hours, but the bulk of our teams won't be in place until tomorrow morning."

Creed rises from the couch. "Well, we don't have any indication of when this attack might start. Maybe we'll be lucky and Ruic and his men are comprehensive in wanting to gather intel. The longer they wait the better it is for us."

"The only problem with that," Doc says, "is that in all the times that things have gone FUBAR around us we've never been lucky."

I stand and look at Lukas and Tundra. "Looks like we're the Amberloq three, fellas. Let's get the king back to the castle and start locking shit down."

Brant nods. "I've got an idea going forward. Lukas is right, the distance between the castle and this place is prohibitive in an emergency. I get that you don't want to create something as accessible as a portal into your home but I think I have another idea. If you guys can spare me for a few hours, I'd like to work in the security office and see if I can locate Yarko and Rowan. It wouldn't hurt to have a couple of travelers on our side."

"On our side being the important part of that sentence, Bear," Hawk says. "That Forest Lord has proven himself to be self-serving."

"Except for where Yarko is concerned," Calli says.

Brant nods. "Rowan won't be winning any awards for altruism, but he seems to have a moral compass. More importantly, both of them can portal in and out of firefights and sticky situations when an emergency evac is needed."

Hawk nods. "No argument there. Okay, you put out some feelers while the rest of us brace for impact."

It dawns on me that I'm the Guardian of the Crown and these men are making all the tactical decisions. Part of being a good leader is to know when to listen, but another part of being a leader is that I have to lead.

"As much as I appreciate all your help, and believe your input is invaluable, the only way the Dornte citizens will put their faith in the Amberloq is if Tundra, Dune, Lukas, and I start heading up the security of the realm. I'm not trying to block you or your help in any way, I just need these decisions to start coming through me and my Generals."

Hawk dips his chin and smiles. "Our resources and expertise are at your disposal, Princess. We're happy to follow your lead, but rest assured, if things go sideways and something threatens our child of fire, the Phoenix Quint will burn this rebellion to the ground."

"Hells yeah we will," Brant growls. "Fun's fun until someone comes at our cub. Then all bets are off."

"Easy boys," Calli says, flashing her men a patient smile. "I've seen this girl in action with her back against the wall. Honor is completely capable of taking on these one-percenter assholes and protecting Creed's crown."

Calli's reassurance goes a long way to bolstering my confidence. In the ten years of segmented time I spent in her life, I was sure of myself and what I had to do. All I need to do is to get back in that frame of mind and I can rock this.

I scan the community room, searching the faces of family, friends, and lovers. The biggest difference between then and now is that I was alone then. I was on the run from Laryssa and had no idea if my plan would work or if I would be betrayed at any moment and fail.

I don't have those worries now.

The team members at my side are solid: the Phoenix Quint, Creed and his mates, and me and mine. We've got the strength and skills to dig in and hold the course.

All we need now is the time to do it.

Sadly, something tells me time is running out.

~

Lukas

We get everyone back to the castle with no issues and then escort Creed, Keyla, Doc, Calli, Kotah, Jaxx, Shadow, and Moonshade to the royal residence to lock down for the next twenty-four hours. Knowing there is trouble on the horizon, we decide everyone should stay within the King's Tower until the full force of our FCO army arrives in the morning.

What we don't want is for some of our numbers to be stuck at Amberloq Hall, while others are in the heirs' suite, and others still are in the King's Tower.

This way, if an attack does ensue in the next few hours, we'll know where everyone is.

Well, everyone except Dune.

Despite what Tundra says, it's obvious he's more anxious about Dune's safety as each hour passes. He should've returned by now. We all know and agree on that, but what we don't know is where he is or what's keeping him.

There's nothing to be done about that now anyway.

As far as we know, he is safe, so we stay focused on what we're dealing with here at the castle.

The security room is busy as we expand and work on our designated tasks. Brant is reaching out and leaving word for Yarko to check in if he gets a chance.

Hawk is checking on the arrival of the first wave of enforcers and arranging for transit shuttles to bring them to the castle from the Dornte Portal Hub.

Rhylan is finishing a video call with his man on the inside at the Breard mint. He's going to let us know if the goblins make any overt moves to suggest they're about to take the economy hostage.

And Tundra is tracking a lead about someone hearing gunfire near the border to the fringe.

"How are you doing, magic man?"

I open my arms to my beautiful soulmate and pull her in for an infusion of strength. "There are certainly things I would rather be doing, but all things considered, we're in pretty good shape. I don't want to jinx us, but I think we've got our bases covered. It's all a matter of time now."

She eases back from me and places a chaste kiss on my lips. "I'm with you on wishing we were doing other things but since we're not, I guess we should talk about our next steps."

"What were you thinking?"

"I'm not as familiar with security dos and don'ts but is there a way to route intel from the war table and this office into a secured access port in the cloud or to a remote location?"

"Probably. How are you hoping that helps us?"

"Well, if we had something like that, if we ever get locked out of the castle again, as we did with Laryssa, we wouldn't be blocked and running blind."

"I've been working on that very thing," Rhylan says joining us. "I wanted to talk to you about it first. Like any backdoor, if it falls into the wrong hands instead of being an asset it has the potential to become a liability."

"I hear what you're saying, and I agree, but if the access was super limited and highly secured, it might be worth the risk. At least in the short-term."

The idea of the short-term gives me an idea. "So, we set it up with the window of access knowing that if anything should happen, we only have a very short time to access it. Conversely, if we're forced out or captured by Ruic's men, we simply hold out until we're sure the window is closed."

Rhylan seems to consider that. "I'm with you, as long as the circle of access is small enough that we're sure the information will be guarded for that needed amount of time."

"You're thinking torture," Honor says.

Rhylan nods. "Goblins are known to be nasty foes and Ruic

is nastier than most. If I set this up, I'd want to ensure those carrying access won't fold under pressure."

"Agreed," I say.

Honor has great instincts and I'm pleased she's stretching herself and assuming her position. "All right, let's do it this way then. Lukas, Tundra, and I will be the primaries, and then you and Hawk will be included as well. That way, access is in the hands of the Amberloq, the Crown, and the Phoenix Quint if necessary."

"And with the five of us, there's no worry of anyone caving. We've all been tortured at one point or another, and certainly can wait out any window if it means protecting the Dornte Crown."

"And fucking over the enemy," Hawk says, grinning as he joins the last of the conversation.

Rhylan nods. "Give me twenty minutes to write the code and set the parameters. Then we'll be good to go."

Before Rhylan steps away, Honor catches his wrist and gives him her full attention. Rhylan stiffens, but I don't think he needs to be guarded.

Sure they've been through a lot—and none of it good—but things have been different lately. Honor's in a good place... even in a bad time.

"Thank you, Dragon. You've been an anchor to quadrant security and we're lucky to have you on our side. One of these days, I'm going to kick your ass for making my life miserable for two years, but other than a black eye coming your way, we're good. I'm over it."

The surprise on Rhy's face is quickly won over by relief. "That's very generous of you, Princess. I swear your forgiveness won't go to waste. And yeah, if a shot to the face settles things, I'll take the hit with a smile on my face. Let me know where and when."

CHAPTER EIGHTEEN

Tundra

I finish questioning the memory sprite who called in about the gunfire and rip the page off my notepad. "I realize this might not be the time to strike off to the four corners of the quadrant, but from what this woman was telling me, I'm wondering if we've discovered the location of a rebel shooting range."

Lukas turns from his conversation with Rhylan and Hawk and lifts his chin in question. "What makes you think that, Iceman?"

"It was the way she described the sound of the shots fired. The ammunition from your realm sounds nothing like the laser bolts or the blaster fire from ours. It got me thinking that if Hunter brought guns into our realm, the rebel forces might need to practice with them before they engage."

"Choosing a warehouse in the fringe lands would be an optimal place to do that," Rhylan says. "Not only is it more remote to hide the sound, but the people there also tend not to live by the same rules as our society."

Hawk frowns. "You're right about it not being a great time to divide our forces, but if there's a chance we've found the depot where they're storing the guns we might be able to stop this rebellion before it starts."

"That's my thinking too," I say, shifting my gaze to the princess. "Let me fly out there and see what I can find out. Then we'll know if we should move in or not."

"How about this?" Honor says. "The first wave of Hawk's FCO enforcers is due to arrive from the other realm within five minutes. If Hawk is agreeable, he, Lukas, and as many men as can fit on his helicopter can accompany you. If this is the depot where the guns are being held, I want them out of rebel hands and destroyed."

Hawk nods. "I can make that happen."

"Here, before you go." Rhylan hands each of us a silver chain with a pendant depicting the fae symbol for peace. "If you snap the pendant at the V, the data port will plug into any localized system. I programmed the access to close in forty-eight hours and will continue to reprogram them as we go forward."

I accept the chain and loop it over my head. After tucking it under my battle vest, I check in with Hawk and Lukas.

Hawk finishes with his pendant and tucks it beneath his fine, knit top. "Ready to roll. Are you coming with us, Bear?"

Brant hangs up his phone and lumbers his massive frame over to join us. It's very rare in life that I feel small next to someone. Being almost seven feet tall, few people meet me eye-to-eye. But even though I still have an inch or two on Brant, he's got me on bulk. He's one hulk of a man. "Yeah, sure, I'm coming. Where are we going?"

"We're taking the helicopter to check out a possible weapons depot on the edge of the fringe."

The massive wildling nods, an easy smile on his face. "Sounds like fun. Shotgun."

I watch as Lukas, Hawk, and Brant get themselves ready to

leave. The three of them have a natural energy and flow I hope to one day share. From what I know, Lukas and Hawk have been a team for years, decades even. Brant was only introduced to the group when Calli resurrected as the phoenix five months ago.

Knowing that gives me hope that six months from now I might not feel like the odd man out in my destiny.

"Be safe you two." Honor meets Lukas and me in the corridor outside the security office. "Don't take any unnecessary chances and watch each other's backs. Ruic is an underhanded asshole. If it comes down to him or you, take him off the board and we'll deal with the fallout later."

"Don't look so worried, babe," Lukas says leaning in to claim her mouth. "This is our wheelhouse. We've got this."

Honor kisses him and then eases back to look at me. "Make sure you use that protective shield of yours to keep yourself safe and to watch out for him."

"You have nothing to worry about. I have no intention of being stripped from your life when we're just getting started. There are so many things I'm looking forward to."

Honor's smile is warm and genuine and when I pull her against my chest her body sways into my embrace with an ease and trust that makes my heart soar.

I take the opportunity to kiss her as a mate should, letting her know how deeply invested I am in our pairing. It may be new, but it's developing, and it's precious to me. "Be well, Princess. And if Dune makes his way back here, make sure you stay close to him. Like you said, we need to keep those protective shields of ours around the people we love."

"I'll remember." She reaches up on her toes to give me one last kiss. "Hurry home and good luck."

❧

Honor

When the guys leave, Rhylan and I get back to work. I've learned to respect the dragon's thoroughness in thinking through the problems coming at us. While I understand he and his twin were primarily the muscle for Laryssa, thankfully, she highly undervalued what he could have contributed to her reign.

"Can you show me how to access the street cameras around Breard Industries?" I ask standing over the console of the municipal security systems.

"Sure, what are you looking for?" He rounds the war table and strides across the floor to meet me at the computer terminal that deals with Dornte infrastructure. "It's a standard grid set up. You log into the system you want, select street cameras, then the live feed, then target a building or an intersection. Once that loads, open the legend on the side and narrow your search parameters."

I watch his fingers dance over the glossy screen. He calls up the destination with little effort.

He is an impressive guy.

"I'm sorry this life cost you your relationship with your twin. I know you were close with him, and I know what it would do to me to find myself on such opposite sides from Creed. I don't know the whole story, and it's none of my business, but for what it's worth, I think you made the right choice."

Rhylan dips his chin and meets my gaze. "When your mother and your brother choose to attend your torture and execution celebration instead of standing up for you, it breaks the part of you that was bonded. I love Creed. Don't ever doubt that. He and I and Keyla and Dillan are so good together it makes me ache. I lost Vik and my mother and even if we find our way back, we'll never be as close as we were, but the trade-off was no loss. My mates are my life, now and forever."

As a mind guardian, there are moments when I'm so focused on a conversation a person's mental energy vibrates with resonance. It's almost like reading his mind.

As Rhylan speaks about my brother and his mates, I not only hear the words he says, but I feel their truth deep to the warmth of his soul.

"I'm glad it worked out for the four of you. I'll consider myself lucky if my mating ends up with the same level of devotion."

"It will, Princess. It's not always easy, but it is always worth it."

I nod and turn my attention back to the screen. "Okay, Breard Industries. What did your inside man say about Ruic's intentions with our economy? Does he believe the goblin will try to assume control that way?"

"He does. He's just not sure when."

I'm guessing it's going to be at some point during a full moon, but that doesn't help. "How much of the quadrant's currency is physical versus digital? If we had to take control of the banking and finance aspect of Dornte's economy could we do it without being in control of the physical money?"

"Creed asked me a similar question the other day. When we looked into it, we realized there are still quite a few primary businesses within the quadrant that deal only in cash since the Wars of Power. The crown can't negate the money without negatively impacting our major industries."

"So, Ruic has us then."

Rhylan tips his head from side to side. "He has leverage over us, for sure, but if Hawk and Creed can sell the idea of a common currency and convince Clarinta, Travon, Rames, and StoneHaven to get on board, we can reclaim that power."

The building I'm staring at on the screen is buzzing with workers going in and out. Breard Industries is on shift change, the day shift leaving for the day, the night shift just arriving.

"I want to be there when the universal currency becomes reality. I have detested that man since I was a teenager and he used to stare at me at my father's parties. I look forward to seeing his face when we finally get to put him in his place."

Rhylan nods. "Then let's put our heads together to find a way to put him in his place."

"Yes. Let's."

~

Lukas

The Dornte Portal Hub is abuzz with early evening commuters when we meet the FCO enforcers. As they come through the portal, we select the five who will add to our numbers in the helicopter, another four who can fly due to their fae species, and send the rest to return to Thornebane Castle.

The squadron leaders heading to secure Creed and the crown are given the contact information for Rhylan and Honor, the arrival information of the next wave, and are introduced to the shuttle driver who will take them back to the castle.

With that taken care of, the thirteen of us jog around to the back of the property and start arming ourselves before we load into Hawk's Eurocopter Dauphin.

"How long will it take us to get there?" Hawk asks Tundra as he gives me the coordinates of the depot. "And which quadrant boundary will we be nearing?"

"We're headed toward the fringe boundary bordering Rames, but we won't be close to the other quadrant. The fringe is quite a vast area of land, and then beyond that are the badlands. We'll still be very much within Dornte territory."

"And how long?" Brant asks.

"I'm unfamiliar with how fast your mechanical bird can fly, but it will take me close to an hour to get there."

I open the cockpit door, climb into the pilot's seat, and get my headset and mic set on. "Well, I plan on following your lead unless something happens, so an hour sounds about right."

"Are we going straight in?" Brant asks. "Or are we landing at a distance and going in with stealth?"

I look to Hawk to gauge his feelings on that. "I think we should land the chopper before getting too close. There aren't helicopters in this realm and after our adventure taking down the dragons, our enemies might be aware we're coming if they hear the rotors."

"Those of us in flight," Tundra says, "won't have that problem. By the time we get there, it will be full dark and our flight is silent."

Hawk nods. "Yeah, that's what I'm thinking too. I think we'll land, and you and your airborne team can do an aerial sweep for intel. We'll make our way on foot and you can catch up with us and brief us on what we're dealing with."

"Understood," Tundra says. "Going forward, it would be advantageous to have comms to link us for communication during flight."

"Oh, we've got you covered there. I've got spare comm' sets in the helicopter. They'll work for infiltration, but odds are you won't be able to hear us over the noise of the helicopter while in flight. I'll grab those for you and yours."

Hawk strides off to grab those out of the cabin of the chopper and leaves Tundra and me to ourselves. He extends his hand, and I clasp it. "Be safe, mate, and if your mechanical bird fails, jump free and I will catch you."

Hawk barks a laugh as he returns but I take the comment as it was meant. Tundra doesn't understand helicopters and is genuinely concerned for my safety.

I slide out of the pilot's seat and pull him in for a hug. It's a little awkward to hug a seven-foot-tall man with a full set of feathered wings, but I'll get the hang of it. "I'll be fine. I've probably got as many hours in the air flying mechanical birds as you have with your wings. Don't be nervous... but thank you for caring."

"Saddle up," Brant says, patting the semiautomatic slung across his chest. "Enough of the sappy shit. Let's do this."

Shadow

"Moonshade, no baby girl. Don't chew that." I shift to the front of my seat on the couch and point across the room. "She's got someone's guitar in her mouth and is chewing the turnkeys."

"Oh dear." Dillan and Keyla both jump off the couch and rush across the room. "No, no, silly girl." Dillan picks her up and hands her off to Keyla. "You don't want to chew that. Why don't you chew the yummy treats we got you?"

"Is your guitar okay?" Keyla asks.

Doc chuckles. "It's fine. I grew up in a foster home of bears. Young bears have terrible tempers. It's not the first time something of mine got damaged from leaving it lying around."

I stand, trying to make out how badly the instrument has suffered, but Moonshade is looking in every direction. "You didn't leave it lying around. You set it down in your own home. My sincere apologies."

"S'all good, counsellor. There are a few little teeth marks in the wood, but no damage done. It's nothing more than a bit of added character."

"Pass it here, Doc," Jaxx says, reaching across the space. "I feel a song or two coming on."

Calli chuckles. "When do you *not* feel a song or two coming on?"

Jaxx flashes her a sexy grin. "When I feel something else coming on."

She bursts out laughing. "That's my Texas jungle cat. Driven by all the urges."

A long, rolling purr fills the air and Moonshade lets off a low growl. "Don't fight the urges. Life's too short to deny yourself the things you crave."

"Speaking of cravings," Calli says. "Any chance the castle kitchen is still open and making pizzas?"

"Likely not the castle kitchen," Creed says, "but Keyla and Doc stocked up on your favorite frozen pizzas. We can put a couple in the oven for you."

"Better make it three," Calli says. "By the time it heats up and the air fills with cheesy goodness, everyone will want a slice. I've learned the hard way if I want to keep this baby fed around wildlings, I need to think ahead."

Keyla laughs and heads toward me with my ebony wolf pup in her hands. "Shadow and I will take our little mischief-maker to the kitchen and get the pizza party started. I gotta keep my baby niece fed."

"Thanks, girlfriend," Calli says, jumping up to join us. "I'll come too. I'll need to snack while we wait."

Keyla chuckles and hands me my pup. "You take her and practice. I'll hold your elbow to make sure you don't crash into anything."

"It's very disorienting."

"I bet it is. You'll get the hang of it soon, I'm sure."

I hope so. Holding Moonshade in front of me, I face her out and work on using her eyes to maneuver my way through the suite.

"Fuckety-fuck," Calli says, her voice tight.

The room turns, all eyes on our phoenix. She's standing frozen in place, looking at the floor. "Oh, no. Did Moonshade leave a mess on the floor?"

"It wasn't Moonshade."

"What is it, kitten?" Jaxx says, jumping to his feet. "Did you drop something? I can pick it up if you can't reach your toes."

Calli meets his gaze, her eyes wide. "I sorta dropped something. You know how we weren't sure how long a phoenix pregnancy lasts? Either my water just broke, or I totally just peed all over the floor."

Everyone in the room is on their feet and rushing around the couches.

"*Chigua*, are you all right? Are you in any pain?" Kotah places a gentle hand on her belly and even from across the room, I can feel the flood of his comforting essence flipping into overload.

"I'm fine, sweetie. Really. Not even a twinge or tingle. I'm just embarrassed about flooding Creed's lovely new hardwood."

Creed waves that away. "Don't worry about that. Doc, what do we do?"

Doc grins at all of us looking frantic. "The first thing we're going to do is relax. Babies get born. It's fine. No one needs to panic."

That seems to settle everyone down a little.

"Next, we're going to get ready for a long night. Jaxx and Shadow go start the pizzas because Calli will need to carb load. Keyla, take her to the shower in her room and stay close while she cleans up. I'll grab her a hospital johnny and meet you in the bedroom for a quick exam to see where we are. Kotah, you and Creed work on letting the others know what's happening. Once that's all taken care of, we'll hunker down and wait for baby Liza to arrive."

"Let the games begin," Jaxx says, looking pale. "What was my job again? I already forgot."

CHAPTER NINETEEN

Honor

*I*t's nearly eight o'clock by the time Rhylan and I fall into a productive rhythm in the security office. Once I started working with him instead of resenting him, I saw and understood how he has his system set up.

He is quite a strategic thinker.

"What about the lockdown protocols? When Laryssa and her team raided us two years ago the fail-safes did no good at keeping her out of the King's Tower."

"Primarily, that was because she had so many people working with her from inside the castle. Any security system can be diverted if it's turned off or altered from within."

"So how do we make sure that doesn't happen again? I know my father was trusting but he wasn't foolish. If Laryssa could convince people within our Dornte family and community to betray him, what hope have we to ensure that won't happen again? Creed and I haven't even gotten a chance to show what we can do."

"I think the easiest way is to close ranks on who has control of things like the security systems and the castle lockdown protocols. Much like the pendants for remote access, if we keep the most sensitive and crucial clearances within our extended family, we have a better shot at preventing a repeat of the past two years."

"Agreed. So, your mating group, mine, and the quint will hold the keys to the crown and everyone within our Amberloq forces, the castle guards, and below will have no chance of over-riding our systems."

Rhylan nods. "That's the way I see it working best. You and your Crown Generals will run the show. I've got things covered here as a backup. And Hawk and Lukas are solid in realm security and can be our safety net if and when we need them.

I like the sound of that.

One of the mistakes Valorous made was to cut herself off to run the Amberloq as an isolated force. There is strength in numbers and there is wisdom in sharing responsibility with people like we have working with us.

After spending only two days pouring over the Guardian Chronicles, I think I have a better handle on what the Amberloq means than my aunt ever did.

It isn't a private army or a source of ego to be its queen, the Amberloq is a symbol of community strength. When she removed her army from its place here at the castle she effectively disconnected those warriors from their purpose.

I won't make the same mistake.

Rhylan is right. We are incredibly fortunate to have the strength and wisdom we need to secure this quadrant within our family.

My tactical watch vibrates against my wrist and snaps me out of my reverie. I turn the small screen to read the incoming message and gasp. "Ohmygods, Calli's water just broke. Our baby girl is coming."

When Rhylan doesn't respond, I turn to see what has him so preoccupied.

"Did you hear me? Our baby phoenix is on her way into the world."

"Sorry, yeah I heard you, but look at this. It's a little late in the evening to be receiving shipments for the castle, isn't it?"

I join him at the war table and study the screen he's watching. Two large semi-trucks are waiting at the outer gate for security to admit them.

"I don't like it," Rhylan says. "Check with the scheduling manifest to see if we're expecting anything that warrants two trucks."

"You think it's a trojan horse attempt?"

"I don't know what that is, but I think those trucks don't have kitchen supplies in them."

"Sorry. Human Realm reference."

His fingers race over the controls and, in response, the bollard barriers eject from the ground. The hydraulic wedges prevent the trucks from moving forward and activate the castle's first-level lockdown protocols.

He taps the screen and opens a voice link with the security house. "This is Rhylan Silverwing in the castle security office. I activated the barriers due to a credible threat against the castle and the crown. Remain inside your station. I'm sending down—"

Tat-a-tat-a-tat-a-tat.

The gunfight is over before the guards get a chance to draw their weapons. The driver of the truck is hanging out the open window and grins up at the camera.

Our men on the gate are down.

The driver gets out, jogs to the back of the truck, and then armed men start flooding out of the trailer of both trucks.

In a stampede of violent intent, hundreds of intruders

hemorrhage out of hiding, race toward the stone walls, and start scaling the ten-foot barriers.

"Slecking hell... we are under attack."

Rhylan runs to the wall, opens the lockbox, and hits the alarm. As bells start ringing the alert, the castle goes into full lockdown.

Lukas

I land the helicopter in a vacant parking lot half a mile north of the coordinates. The area is incredibly isolated and reminds me of an old American ghost town in a western movie. "I love what they've done to the neighborhood. It's so welcoming."

"And the perfect place to stash guns without being noticed," Hawk adds.

As the sound of the rotors quiets, I finish with my shutdown and the helicopter team gets out to stretch.

"Tundra and the aerial group won't be long I'm sure," I say, locking things up. "We'll hump it that way and they'll meet up with us en route."

Hawk looks over the FCO enforcers with us and gives them a nod. "We appreciate you boys making the trip. We'll treat this like any other op. We go in, assess the surroundings, and react accordingly. This may not be FCO jurisdiction, but we are here at the request of the quadrant king, so that's how we represent ourselves."

I don't doubt their abilities or their ethics.

Our FCO squadrons are the elite of all fae security in the human realm. When Tundra lands with his squadron, our group is complete.

"Are we in the right place?" I ask Tundra.

"I believe so."

"Alrighty then, boys," Brant says, flashing them a winning grin. "You can fill us in on the way. Locked and loaded. Let's ride the tide."

Hawk finishes strapping on his flak jacket, checks his weapon, and we're good to go. "Lukas, you're on point. Brant, you've got the rear. Tundra, you got your team for aerial support. Quick in. Quick out. Let's getter done and get back to the castle."

The group falls in line behind me and we're off.

Two minutes into our approach, my tactical watch buzzes with an incoming message. When Brant and Hawk pause to look at theirs as well, the three of us react at once.

"Seriously? Now?" Brant says.

"What's going on?" Tundra asks.

"Calli's water just broke," Hawk says. "Jaxx says there is no labor so far, but Doc examined her and it's definitely baby time."

"Congratulations," Tundra says. "We will finish this and get you boys home for your baby phoenix."

"Yeah, no thanks," Brant grumbles. "I have no intention of missing the birth of my daughter."

"A first-born labor can take six to twelve hours," I say. "Lots of time to get through this and get back. Besides, Jaxx and Kotah are there, and Doc won't let anything happen to Calli or the baby. We need to keep our heads in the game and check this lead."

Hawk doesn't look happy about it but nods and turns to Tundra. "What did you learn from doing an aerial pass over the location?"

"There's a shooting range set up in the woods behind a barn. We didn't go down to examine the targets but based on the kind of damage we saw, the guns weren't anything from our realm. We believe we're in the right place."

"Good enough," I say. "Fan out and come in from all sides.

Initiate on my mark, gentlemen. Textbook insurgency. Let's do this."

It takes three minutes to get into position. With Hawk, Brant, Tundra, and I each wearing a tactical watch, it's easy to coordinate our insurgence.

Three... two... one...

I give my squadron a hand signal to move in and we make a beeline for the barn at the back of the property. Crouched over in a stealth run, we stick to the darkest shadows to keep from being seen. We cut the distance to the barn within seconds. There's movement inside the barn but with no light, there's nothing we can glean.

I tap the comm in my ear as my team reaches the side door of the barn. "Alpha team in position."

"Delta team in position," Brant replies.

"Beta team in position," Hawk says.

I nod to the demolitions man on my team, and he places two small, explosive discs against the hinges of the side door. "Set blast charges for ten seconds."

"Detonations set, sir."

I nod and he falls back. "Alpha team set to enter."

"Beta set."

"Delta set."

I glance back and we're good to go. "Initiate."

We turn away to shield ourselves from the detonation blast and then roll straight into infiltration. Wood boards splinter and hit the ground in a clatter at our feet but we're already moving in.

The detonation disc blew the door hinges and opened our way. The penetration into the depths of the barn is done with a speed and precision I'm proud of.

FCO enforcers truly are an elite group.

We're twenty feet inside the barn, searching the darkness for hostiles when the high-pitched keening of a detonation trigger sounds.

"Bomb! Fall back!" I barely get the words out when the world explodes into a fiery ball of hell. I must be close to Ground Zero of where the detonation is situated because I'm lifted off the ground and thrown behind a wave of power like I weigh nothing.

I hit the dirt of the barn floor with a thud, my head ringing as my vision fritzes in and out. My wrist buzzes and I force my vision to focus long enough to read the incoming message.

The castle is under attack.

I groan as reality hits. It's no coincidence we got a tip to draw us away from the castle. This is a coordinated effort to divide and conquer.

Fuck me. We need to get back to Honor.

I roll onto my chest and push my palms against the cool packed dirt. Footsteps are thundering in from all directions and I have no idea if they belong to friend or foe. I give it my all to push onto my knees, but the effort is futile. My strength gives out and I faceplant back down into the blood-soaked dirt.

That's not a good sign.

Whose blood is this?

My mind isn't working at full capacity, but I have a bad feeling the answer is obvious. I probe my ear to ensure my comm is still in place and clear my throat. "I think I'm in trouble, boys. Man down."

Tundra

When Lukas shouts that there's a bomb, my world is knocked off its axis. I received this call from the tip line and suggested we come here. I ran the intel sweep and gave the team the okay to proceed. And now I'm hovering in the skies above as the barn erupts into a giant explosion of wood and flames.

It's more than just our men getting ambushed that bothers me. Lukas is in that explosion.

My wrist vibrates and I read the incoming message.

The castle is under attack.

Screw my life.

My duty is to Creed and Keyla first, Honor second, and everyone else after that.

"I think I'm in trouble, boys. Man down." Even over the broken crackle of the comms line, I hear how wrong Lukas's voice sounds.

I have my orders and they aren't to engage with the burning building. Strangely enough, in my moment of panic, it's Dune's voice I hear clearest in my mind. *"There's more to life than duty, Frosty. Sometimes you gotta go with your gut."*

I scan the ground below and spot two dozen enemy troops flooding into the barnyard.

This is one of those times.

I have a duty to the success of the operation, but I have a duty to Lukas too. I also have a duty to Honor and our union. It's not as simple as the textbooks and teachings make it seem. Reality is messy.

With a curse, I dive toward the flames and brace for the searing heat. The barn is old, and the wood is dry. It's going up like a tinderbox and the wave of the inferno is incredible.

I take a deep breath before I'm consumed by the rising flames. The smoke hits my eyes and stings, but there's nothing to be done about that. I need to find Lukas and, in this burning hell, that is a challenge.

"Lukas! Lukas, where are you?"

No sound comes back to me or maybe it does and I don't hear it over the crackling of wood and the snapping of beams above me.

This whole place is about to come down.

The incoming troops don't seem to be advancing into the barn, so I assume they were moving in to capture the members of the team who were dazed by the explosion. I can't worry about that right now.

In this moment, my only concern is Lukas.

Flexing my back, I bring my wings up to shield myself from the heat as I search. It takes a moment for my eyes to adjust to the brilliance of the flames, but I'm starting to make out my surroundings.

A loud crack sounds above me.

One of the support beams is burning through and is about to snap. When that happens, the roof will cave in and we'll both be buried and burned alive.

I need to find him and get out.

I know what door Lukas and his team entered and I make my way to that side of the barn.

I see a man lying face down in the dirt and I rush forward. Black fatigues, muscled physique, military cut black hair...

I drop to my knees to assess—dead.

My heart hammers hard as I flip him over...

It's not him.

I draw an unsteady breath and it strikes me that I shouldn't rejoice over a fallen soldier being dead in Lukas's place. I send the FCO officer my deepest regrets.

Crack.

That crack was louder than the first—

I dive out of the way as a section of the roof comes crashing down. Flaming wood tumbles onto my back and I'm knocked to the ground.

I can't stay down, or I'll burn.

I grunt, pushing against the weight, and roll to get free of the debris. The smoke is thick, making breathing almost impossible. It feels like my lungs are on fire.

I can't leave.

Not yet.

Lukas led his team, so he won't be far from his fallen man. He's not the kind to let others face dangers first. He is close... I know it.

I stay low to the ground and flap my wings to clear the air enough for me to pull in some oxygen. I'm getting dizzy from being buried and the lack of oxygen. I'll be no help to Lukas or anyone else if I die in here too.

There.

I spot another downed man and crawl the short distance to get to him. Rolling him over, I'm both relieved and terrified to find that it's Lukas. He's unconscious and when I ease back, my hands are slick with blood.

Where is he hurt?

I have no time to find out.

Another crack above signals the coming collapse of the entire structure. Gathering Lukas into my arms, I stand, and glance up, searching for a way to get free of this inferno.

I can't see anything but flames.

If I fly straight into the fire and the roof comes down on me, we die. If I wait any longer... we die.

With no choice left but to leave our fate to the whim of the gods, I push off the ground and launch toward the fiery skies above.

CHAPTER TWENTY

Shadow

Something is very wrong in the world around us. Only moments after Calli's water breaks, bells start ringing throughout the suite, and then screens descend over all the windows. Moonshade stiffens in my arms and growls, searching for the source of the strange noise.

"What's happening?" Jaxx asks.

Creed frowns at the wall as all four of the large windows are blocked out by solid sheets of descending metal. "Someone triggered castle lockdown."

The jaguar prowls over to get the last glimpses of the grounds outside before the windows are completely sealed shut. "I assume the windows are supposed to be doing this then?"

"When activated, yes. Rhylan and I had them installed the moment we regained control of the castle to prevent forced entry into the King's Tower."

"And they're bullet and laser proof?"

"They are." Creed rushes out from the great room of the King's Tower and Jaxx and I follow.

By shifting Moonshade in my arms, I find that I am remarkably self-sufficient. Lukas was right. Being bound with a spirit wolf is a rare and incredible honor.

Creed taps the screen of the security console while Jaxx strides toward the door. "It'll be locked," Creed says absently.

"It is."

"Okay, so, the logs say Rhy locked us down from the security office."

"Just us or the entire castle?" Jaxx asks.

"The entire castle."

"Should we call him and find out what's going on?"

Creed shakes his head. "No. If there's trouble, he's busy. He knows I'll want to be informed. He'll call as soon as he gets a chance."

"Jaxx, Dillan needs you." Keyla rushes toward us from the guest rooms at the back of the suite. She's pale and not at all looking like her calm and serene self.

"What's wrong?" the jaguar asks.

"Dillan's not saying in front of Calli, but he gave me a list of things he needs from the castle clinic. I know him. He's worried. Creed, can you call down and have them send it up?"

The answer is written on Creed's face before he speaks a word. "We're on lockdown. While our security teams have the option to move within the castle and the grounds, we don't. We can't get anything or anyone in or out of the King's Tower until twenty-four hours after the lockdown is lifted."

"Twenty-four hours?" Jaxx says. "If Calli's in trouble, twenty-four hours is too late."

Creed looks tormented. "I'm sorry. There's nothing to be done about it. It was one of the security protocols we put in place to avoid another massacre."

"All right," Keyla says, gripping Jaxx's arm. "If there's nothing to be done, we'll make do and handle any issues that arise the same way we always do—together and one challenge at a time."

Jaxx frowns, his muscled frame rigid with tension. "Creed, do what you can to find out what's going on outside these walls. We'll work on replacing the items on Doc's list with things within this suite. Maybe he's being cautious and it's not time to hit the panic button."

"He likely wants to be prepared for all contingencies," I offer.

Keyla nods. "I'm sure that's all it is."

~

Honor

After Rhylan sounds the alarm, and the castle goes into full lockdown, the two of us dive straight into defending Thornebane Castle from the incoming forces. Images appear above the war table, and I study the castle from every angle inside and out.

"Do you think Ruic has men inside the castle?"

"I don't know. I hope not. We've been tough on vetting since Creed took the throne. If there are traitors in our midst, I'm confident there won't be many."

"Enough that we can take them out one by one."

"That's the theory, yeah."

"Shit, there are a lot of them." I watch as the horde of intruders spills across the lawn like a black flood. "Wait... what are those?"

I point to the screen as hundreds of red lights appear on the ground, glowing against the darkness. At first, I think they are laser sprinkler heads rising from the landscaped grass, but then the sprinkler heads start moving.

"Are they drones?"

"They're spider sentinels," Rhy says, switching the cameras to night scope vision to give us a better view. "Hawk had a guy in the human realm who developed them as the first line of defense."

My gaze flips from image to image, watching the sentinels scurry and spread across the manicured grounds of the castle.

"And you can target the incoming force?"

"That's the plan."

Each of the mechanical arachnids has a bright red light on the center of its back but as it approaches a target, green scope lights beam from its head. Where those lights fall, the raiders drop to the ground.

"What are they shooting?"

"It's a combination of a tranq dart and an electroshock to knock them out and paralyze them until we release their muscles in captivity."

"Is that even a thing?"

Rhylan chuckles. "I had the same reaction but one thing you'll learn about Hawk and Lukas is they never joke about military security. Those guys have their fingers on the pulse of everything."

"And according to Calli, Hawk has more money than he knows how to spend, so he loves to shop and develop tech like this."

"I'm sure that's true."

"Have you notified anyone of the attack?"

"No, I've been too busy here but I'm sure everyone in the castle realizes what's going on. Creed accessed the security feeds the moment the alarm sounded, so he knows I locked us down. He also knows he and Keyla are now sealed in the King's Tower for the duration."

"Good. That protects them at least." I pull my tablet from my pocket and message Tundra and Lukas asking for a sit rep on where they are and how their op went.

When that's done, I go back to studying the monitors. "Now

to ensure those forces stay out of our castle until we round them all up."

"I'm tracking the shuttle now to see how far out the next wave of Hawk's men are. If you take over here, I'll round up the ones who already arrived and secure the castle entrances."

I wave off his words. "You know these systems much better than I do. You stay where you're needed, and I'll grab the soldiers and secure the castle. Where are they now?"

"In the main cafeteria getting fed and oriented with a layout of the castle."

"Got it. Now, if we go outside, how do we keep the sentinels from knocking us out?"

"Oh, good question." He rushes to the cubby against the wall and pulls out a bulky package. "These dermal tags carry a frequency the sentinels will recognize as you being a friend and not a foe. Stick it on your skin somewhere it won't get rubbed off and you're good to go."

I take the package and laugh. "Avengers stickers?"

Rhylan rolls his eyes. "Brant was in charge of the design and decided beige or white was boring. He thought these were much better."

"Of course, he did. Awesome, now I can't decide whether I want to be Scarlet Witch or Black Widow."

"Definitely Black Widow. Natasha Romanoff kicks ass and that's who we need you to be."

"You know the Avengers, dragon?"

"Oh, yeah. Dillan and Keyla got Creed and I all caught up on those movies. They're damn good."

"They are." I peel and stick my dermal tag and then head to the door. "Good luck and stay safe. And Rhylan... thanks for being on our side. We're lucky to have you."

With that said, I leave the security office, tablet in hand, and connect my comm access to the castle sound system. When I exit the security door at the bottom of the stairs, I open a voice channel. "Good evening, everyone. As you might have guessed, the rebels are making an offensive strike against the crown. This is not a drill."

I reach the top of the stairs and am saddened by the fear I see in the eyes of our citizens. "Without panicking, move in an orderly fashion to secure yourself in one of the four designated shelter areas within the castle. Do not attempt to go outside. Counter-insurgency measures have been activated and we don't want any of you injured."

Knowing that running inspires panic, I walk briskly toward the main cafeteria. "Your king and queen are safe and our forces are many. What happened two years ago will never happen again. We are ready this time. Dornte will never again fall to tyranny."

As if the universe is intent on proving me wrong, a loud crash rings through the air and glass smashes up ahead. I draw my blaster and break into a run.

I promised these people they would never live in fear again and as long as I have breath in my lungs, no one will take over my brother's crown.

Dune

I soar through the night sky, in no rush to get back. No doubt Tundra returned long before now. He probably took one efficient look around the Snowy Peaks Biome, came to some kind of intelligent reasoning, and raced straight back to dutifully give his report.

There's no way he spent the entire day curled up at the base of a desert willow wallowing in old memories of his glory years. As a child, I was a favorite among my people. As a warrior, I brought them pride. As a man, I was known to be a gifted lover and life of the party.

Why did I leave?

Life beyond the Desert Planes never treated me half as well. And now there's no going back. The life I loved so dearly is gone forever.

The people I loved... all gone.

Learning the Elbirfae were exterminated makes me even less qualified to be an Amberloq General. When I was the most qualified desert warrior, I convinced myself I had a place here representing my biome.

Tundra and I are the last two of our species.

That means to rebuild the forces to guard the crown, Elbirfae are now the minority and not the power. As much as I argued the point my people should remain the protectors of the crown, that can no longer be the case.

It's a sad day in the history of Dornte.

Is it wrong that I didn't want to return to face it?

After Tundra broke the bad news, they probably started an all-out scramble to figure out what to do next. With Lukas's security training, Tundra's knowledge of the quadrant protocols, and Honor's contacts as the Guardian of the Crown, they're an Amberloq super team.

They don't need me.

I close my eyes and let the cool breeze of night soothe my aching heart. It doesn't fix anything, but Honor's right... there's something about flying that feeds the soul.

Honor's been right about a lot of things.

She's the main reason I came back. Whether she meant it or not, she said she sees something in me. I've got no one else on my side. I might as well try to live up to her expectations.

Except... I know that won't last long.

In the end, everyone gets fed up with me.

As I draw near, I scan the scenery below. Thornebane Castle

is lit up like a laser light show, and I drop lower to get a better look.

What the—?

The grounds are swarming with mechanical spiders and men dropping like timber planks in every direction.

What the slecking hell is happening?

I don't want to land in the midst of the chaos without knowing what's going on. I certainly don't want to be hit with whatever projectiles are felling soldiers like trees in the woods.

I pump my wings, arch my back, and return to the shadowed sky as I continue to Amberloq Hall.

The windows on all four floors of the mansion are glowing gold against the night. There are armed men standing sentinel at the iron gate, in front of the porch steps, and on all four corners of the building.

Are they our men or an opposing force?

There's no way Honor raised an army since I've been gone. It hasn't even been two days.

But Hawk has men...

That thought fires me up and adrenaline fuels my flight. Were we attacked? Are Honor and Tundra all right? Are Creed and the Crown of Dornte secured?

There are too many unknowns to simply drop in at the front door. *Hi, honey, I'm home.*

No. Despite what people think, I'm far more strategic than that. I'll let myself in and see what I'm dealing with before I announce myself.

If Honor hadn't shared the information with me, I wouldn't know where the oculus room was or how it works. But I do. Hunkering down in the safety of the rotunda will allow me a moment to regroup and reassess instead of walking straight through the front doors.

I stay high in the air and out of the moon's light for as long as I can. When I'm directly over the oculus window, I straighten in the air, raise my wings over my head, and plummet feet-first toward the mansion.

Wind whistles in my ears but I don't flare my wings to break my fall until after the glass eye of the ceiling spins and opens to offer me entry.

Emergency lights come on with the motion sensor and I stride over to input my access code into the house monitoring system. I hope it's on the same circuit as downstairs or I'm screwed. I push in my digits and the security screens pop to life. One by one I get a look at the rooms downstairs and I scan through the faces.

I don't recognize one person down there.

What the hell is going on?

Author Notes

Written on 09/27/2021

Ah... that ended a bit cliffy. Sorry about that, I usually wrap up better between books but so much is happening. Stay with me, I promise it'll be worth it. Things are heating up and the five mates are set. Now to see how they handle the challenge of a quadrant in turmoil.

I hope you're enjoying the continuation of the Guardians of the Fae Realms through the love story of Honor, Lukas, Shadow, Tundra, and Dune.

Don't miss what happens next with Honor as she finds her footing with her mates and begins to restore the Amberloq forces. Grab Honor Bound, the third book in Honor's harem here.

As always, if you want to check in with me, I welcome the chance to chat. I'm active on FB and pretty good at getting to my emails.

Hugs to all,

JL

Find Me

My Direct Sales Site: Shopify

My books

Web page – www.jlmadore.com

Email – jlmadorewrites@gmail.com

Newsletter – JL Series Updates

HONOR BOUND

The rebellion has started. The goblins are coming for us. My time to prepare is over.

The battle for the Dornte crown has begun and we're not ready. Ruic Breard has an army, a stockpile of weapons from the Human Realm, and the knowledge that the Amberloq force consists of two Elbirfae warriors, and me. Go team!

What our enemies don't know is that Dune, Tundra, and I have a support network behind us... the Phoenix Quint, the Thornebane Quad, and most importantly, my wildcard mates, Lukas and Shadow.

Oh, and don't forget sweet Moonshade.

To win this struggle for power and control once and for all, and to save the Dornte quadrant from another reign of tyranny, my mates and I have to unite and embrace our shared destiny as Guardians of the Crown.

Claim your copy of now: **Honor Bound**

ALSO BY JL MADORE

Book 1 – Captured by the Magi

Book 2 – Jesse and the Magi Vault

Book 3 – The Makings of a Magi Knight

Book 4 – Clash with the Magi Council

Book 5 – The Unstoppable Storme

Club Sanguine

Book 1 – Moonstone Maelstrom

Book 2 - Sunstone Sacrifice

JL's More Traditional M/F, M/M, or Menage

The Watchers of the Gray Series (Paranormal)

Book 1 – Watcher Untethered – Zander

Book 2 – Watcher Redeemed – Kyrian

Book 3 – Watcher Reborn – Danel

Book 4 – Watcher Divided – Phoenix

Book 5 – Watcher United – Seth

Book 6 – Watcher Compelled – Bo

Book 7 – Watcher Unfeigned – Brennus

Book 8 – Watcher Exposed – Taharqa

The Scourge Survivor Series (Fantasy)

Book 1 – Blaze Ignites

Book 2 – Ursa Unearthed

Book 3 – Torrent of Tears

Book 4 – Blind Spirit

Book 5 – Fate's Journey

Book 6 – Savage Love – epilogue novella

Aliens of Atlantis Series (Sci-Fi)

Book 1 – Taryn's Tiderider

Book 2 – Kai's Captive

Book 3 – Alyandra's Shadow